"Der... I'm...
bu...

"I wa...
enti...

Desire flooded my body, rushing through my veins, awakening every nerve ending. The silence stretched between us for long seconds while my mind raced with uncertainty. "I..." I swallowed and tried again, not entirely sure what words might tumble out of my mouth. "I...excuse me."

I escaped to the bathroom, closed the door behind me and leaned against it. I stared at myself in the mirror, touched my skin, my hair, concrete things that defined me. But what about the things I couldn't see...those deep, dark desires that lurked in my heart? Those things defined me, too, whether I liked it or not.

I didn't like it, knowing that my body could override my reason. But I couldn't help but acknowledge how much I wanted Redford, how much I wanted to share his bed tonight. Worse, how much I needed to share his bed.

So with shaking hands I slipped my engagement ring from my finger and set it on the vanity. Then I opened the door, inhaled deeply and walked out into the bedroom...to my husband.

Dear Reader,

We all slip up sometime—we stumble, then recover and, hopefully, learn something in the process. But what if you can't get over the biggest mistake of your life?

Denise Cooke married U.S. Marine Redford DeMoss three years ago in a quickie Vegas wedding after a whirlwind courtship. Their honeymoon was mind-boggling, but when Redford returned to his overseas duty and Denise returned to NYC, reality set in, and she had the marriage annulled. Except now she's being reunited with her biggest mistake to resolve a tax issue and Redford looks better than ever...can she keep from making the same mistake twice?

Continuing with the characters I first introduced in "The Truth about Shoes and Men" on www.eHarlequin.com and in the Harlequin Temptation novel *Cover Me, My Favorite Mistake* is a sexy romp about two mismatched lovers who begin to suspect that that the only thing worse than living with each other is living *without* each other. I hope you enjoy this book as much as I enjoyed writing it! Visit me at my Web site, www.stephaniebond.com. And please tell your friends about the wonderful love stories within the pages of Harlequin romance novels!

Much love and laughter,

Stephanie Bond

Books by Stephanie Bond

HARLEQUIN BLAZE
2—TWO SEXY!

HARLEQUIN TEMPTATION

Stephanie Bond

my favorite mistake

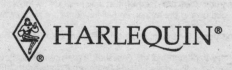

HARLEQUIN®

TORONTO • NEW YORK • LONDON
AMSTERDAM • PARIS • SYDNEY • HAMBURG
STOCKHOLM • ATHENS • TOKYO • MILAN • MADRID
PRAGUE • WARSAW • BUDAPEST • AUCKLAND

ISBN 0-373-79173-9

MY FAVORITE MISTAKE

Copyright © 2005 by Stephanie Bond Hauck.

www.eHarlequin.com

Printed in U.S.A.

Dear Reader,

An Evening To Remember... Those words evoke all kinds of emotions and memories. How do you plan a romantic evening with your guy that will help you get in touch with each other on every level?

Start with a great dinner that you cook together. Be sure to light several candles and put fresh flowers on the table. Enjoy a few glasses of wine and pick out your favorite music to set the mood. After dinner take the time to really talk to each other. Hold hands and snuggle on the sofa in front of the fireplace. And maybe take a few minutes to read aloud selected sexy scenes from your favorite Harlequin Blaze novel. After that, anything can happen....

That's just one way to have an evening to remember. There are so many more. Write and tell us how you keep the spark in your relationship. And don't forget to check out our Web site at www.eHarlequin.com.

Sincerely,

Birgit Davis-Todd
Executive Editor

This book is dedicated to the memory of
Cheryl Anne Porter, a sister Harlequin writer
who could light up a room with her smile
and leave your ribs aching from laughing.
You will be missed, Cheryl.

1

"THIS IS A MISTAKE," I said, suddenly panicked by the horde of women pushing at me from all sides. In the minutes just prior to Filene's Basement "running of the brides," the crowd was getting hostile, all elbows and bared teeth.

Next to me, my friend Cindy turned her head and scowled. "Denise Cooke, you can't back out now—I'm counting on you!" The normally demure Cindy Hamilton shoved a woman standing next to her to make room to reach into her shoulder bag. "Here, put on this headband so we can spot each other once we get in there."

I sighed and reached for the neon pink headband. It wasn't as if I could look more ridiculous—I was already freezing and humiliated standing there in my yoga leotard (the Web-site-recommended uniform for trying on bridal gowns in the aisles). February in New York did not lend itself to leotards—I was numb from my V-neck down. "This is a lot of trouble for a discounted wedding gown when you're not even engaged," I grumbled.

"This was your idea, Miss Penny Pincher," Cindy reminded me.

That was true. I was helping Cindy with her Positive Thinking 101 class, and her assignment was to prepare for an event with the idea being that it would then become a self-fulfilling prophecy. Since Cindy wanted to be married more than anything else in the world, she'd decided to buy a wedding gown. Cheapskate that I am (an investment broker-slash-financial planner, actually), I had suggested Filene's biannual bridal event for a good deal.

So here we were at seven-thirty on a cold Saturday morning, poised with oh, about eight or nine hundred other freezing leotard-clad women, waiting for the doors of Filene's to be hurled open. There were a few identifiable teams with members wearing identical hats or T-shirts. Like me, they were friends who had been commandeered to grab as many dresses as possible from the clearance racks, thereby increasing the odds of the bride-to-be getting a gown she wanted.

"Remember," Cindy said, her eyes as serious as an NFL coach dispensing plays, "strapless or spaghetti straps, with a princess waistline—white is my first choice, but I'm willing to go as far left as light taupe. I need a size ten, but I can work with a twelve."

I nodded curtly. "Got it."

"If you find a gown that might work, put it on so no one can grab it out of your hands."

I swallowed and nodded again, suddenly apprehensive.

"And who knows," Cindy added with a grin. "You might find a dress that you'll want to keep for yourself."

I frowned. "Barry and I haven't even talked about getting married."

"Good grief, you've been dating for two years— he's going to propose someday, and then you'll already have a dress. It's *practical*."

I started to say it was presumptuous, then remembered why Cindy was there and clamped my mouth shut. Barry was...great, but I couldn't see myself getting married...again.

Like every time I remembered my last-minute and short-lived Las Vegas marriage to Sergeant Redford DeMoss, I got a sick feeling in my stomach. My first marriage was one of those events in my life that I wanted to expunge from my memory, like a stupid teenage stunt...except I hadn't been a stupid teenager—I had been a stupid adult. In the three years since my marriage to and subsequent annulment from Redford, I had managed to block the incident from my mind for the most part. But since two of my best friends, Jacki and Kenzie, had recently gotten married and my last single friend, Cindy, seemed hell-bent on doing the same, the memories of my incredible wedding night had been popping into my head at the strangest moments—I couldn't seem to outrun them.

Someone behind me stepped on my heel, scraping it raw. I winced, not sure how I was going to outrun this dogged bunch, either.

"They're opening the doors," Cindy announced excitedly.

A cheer rose from the crowd and everyone lurched forward collectively. The two security guards unlocking the doors looked as frightened as I felt. When the doors were flung open, self-preservation kicked in—I had to match the pace of the crowd or be trampled. I squeezed through the double doors and ran for the escalator, my heart pounding in my chest. The escalator was instantly jammed, and everyone still clambered upward, some screaming as if we were all vying for front row seats at a rock concert. At the top of the escalator, we spilled onto the second floor where several freestanding racks bulged with pouf dresses. I had no idea where Cindy was and I hesitated, not sure where to begin.

Women stampeded by me in a blur and began yanking dresses by the armfuls from the rack. It was a locust swarm. I realized I was going to miss out if I didn't move quickly. Cindy's order of "strapless or spaghetti straps" vanished in the wake of the disappearing gowns. I grabbed whatever I could get my hands on, draping the gowns over my shoulders until I could barely see or hear past the mounds of rustling fabric.

Within one minute, the racks had been picked clean. As if on cue, everyone began trying on dresses where they stood, stripping to their underwear and in some cases, even further, heedless of the male salesclerks and security guards milling about. Keeping an eye out for a neon pink head-band, I sorted through my spoils like a lion pro-tecting its kill.

I had managed to snare a white satin gown with cap sleeves, size fourteen; an off-white long-sleeved lacy number with a straight skirt, size twenty; a pinkish Gibson-girl design with bishop sleeves, size twelve; a dark beige high-neck gown with an embroidered bodice, size four; and a creamy halter-style gown with a pearl-studded skirt, size ten. My shoulders fell in disappointment—I had struck out for Cindy.

Although…the halter-style gown was actually quite nice. I peered at the designer label and my eye-brows shot up—*really* nice. Then I peered at the price tag and my eyebrows practically flew off my head—a $2000 gown reduced to $249? Cindy would be crazy not to buy this dress, even if it wasn't ex-actly what she was looking for. While juggling the other gowns, I stepped into the halter dress and twisted to zip it up in the back, then smoothed a hand over the skirt, reveling in the nubby texture of the seed pearls. Longing welled in my heart, surprising me, because I was the most no-nonsense person I knew—a dress couldn't possibly have any power over me.

"That's perfect on you," said a salesclerk next to me.

"Oh, I'm helping a friend of mine," I replied quickly.

"Pity," the woman said, nodding toward a mir-rored column a few feet away.

I glanced around, looking for Cindy in the frenzied mob, then reasoned I might as well walk past the mirror on my way to find her. I moseyed over and stopped dead in my tracks.

Even over the leotard the dress was dazzling, and for a few seconds, I *felt* dazzling—my makeup-free face and dark blond, disheveled ponytail notwithstanding. For my quickie Vegas wedding, I'd worn a "What Happens Here, Stays Here" T-shirt, which in hindsight, had been a big red flag to my state of mind. I'd told myself a hundred times that it wouldn't have mattered if Redford and I had been married in a lavish church ceremony with all the trimmings; but now, looking at myself in the mirror wearing this glorious gown, I had to admit that the right wardrobe would have lent a touch of sophistication to the surreal occasion.

If I ever married again, I would wear this dress… or something like it.

"Do you have any size sixteens?" a girl yelled in my face. "I need a size sixteen!"

I shook my head, then realized that all around me, women were bartering unwanted gowns, some hoisting signs heralding their size. I relinquished the size four to a peanut-sized woman, and during the handoff, the rest of my bounty was ripped from my arms by circling gown-vultures. I was still reeling when Cindy skidded to a stop in front of me.

"There you are!" she shrieked over the melee. "I found my dress!"

Indeed, over her leotard she wore a sweet, strapless white satin gown with a princess waistline. Laughing like a child, she twirled, sending the full skirt billowing around her.

"It's perfect," I agreed. The dress *was* perfect for Cindy's cherubic beauty, but I felt a pang of sadness as I glanced down at the halter dress I wore…it would have to be sacrificed to the vortex of bargain-hunting brides, which had, if anything, increased in intensity as latecomers descended on the leftovers and another round of frantic stealing and swapping ensued.

Cindy stopped twirling and stared at me. "Wow, that dress looks awesome on you."

I flushed. "I was just trying it on…for you. It was the closest thing I could find."

Cindy's blue eyes bugged. "You should keep it, Denise. If Barry got a look at you in that dress, he'd fall on his knees and beg you to marry him."

I laughed. "Right." Barry had never been on his knees in my presence—to propose or do anything else—but I had to admit, I was tempted.

A flushed, middle-aged woman stopped and looked me up and down. "Are you going to keep that dress?" Without waiting for an answer, she proceeded to pick up the fabric of the skirt to scrutinize the pearls.

A proprietary feeling came over and I firmly removed her hand from my—er, *the* dress. "I haven't decided."

The woman glared at my bare left hand. "My daughter Sylvie already has a wedding date."

I frowned. "So?"

"So," the woman snapped, "what good will that dress do you hanging in your closet?"

She was testy, but she had a very good point, especially considering the fact that I'd been lamenting only yesterday how small my closet was. Still, what business was it of hers if the dress hung in my cramped closet until it dry-rotted? (A distinct possibility.)

Cindy stepped up and crossed her arms. "My friend is going to get married again someday." Cindy still harbored lingering guilt over my impromptu marriage—she blamed herself for getting the flu and leaving me to spend Christmas and New Year's Eve in Las Vegas by myself. Otherwise, I might not have fallen under Redford's illicit spell.

"Again? Someday?" The lady snorted and her body language clearly said that women who didn't get it right the first time around didn't deserve a production the second time around. Another good point. I *had* blown it the first time I'd walked down the aisle—well, okay, to be morbidly honest I hadn't "walked down the aisle." I was married in a chapel drive-through, which, in my defense, had seemed the most economical route at the time.

My groom, who I barely knew, was a gorgeous officer on leave. And the spontaneous marriage had been prompted by intense physical chemistry (Redford was rather spectacularly endowed), and perhaps a bit of misplaced patriotism that I had mistaken for love. It was one of the oldest clichés in the book—an observation which, I realized ruefully, was also a cliché. The biggest mistake of my life was redundant. Ridiculously, tears pooled in my eyes.

Cindy gaped at me. I never cried…*ever.*

"There, there," the older woman said, and actually patted my arm. "You'll feel better once you take off that dress."

Cindy drew herself up. "Keep moving, lady—the dress is ours."

The woman huffed and stalked away, head pivoting, presumably looking for other women she could provoke to tears.

Mortified, I blinked like mad to rid my eyes of the moisture. "I don't know…what happened."

"Never mind," Cindy said in her best-friend voice. "Let's go pay for our dresses."

I shook my head. "I can't buy a wedding dress, Cindy."

"Of course you can…everyone knows you have a fortune squirreled away from clipped coupons and rebates."

I had a reputation among my friends for being, shall I say, "thrifty." "I don't mean I can't afford it. I mean I…I don't think I'll ever get married…again." But if that were true, why hadn't I simply handed over the dress to the pushy woman?

Cindy shrugged. "Fine. If you still feel that way

in six months, sell the dress on eBay. Knowing you, you'll probably make money on it."

I bit my lower lip. Cindy was right—even if I took the dress home, no one was going to stick a gun to my head and make me get married. Barry seemed to be as leery of walking down the aisle as I was. Although if one day Barry got the urge...

I almost laughed out loud—Barry wasn't the "urge getting" kind of guy. He was just as methodical and nonsensical as I was, which explained how we had contentedly dated off and on for the past two years without the drama that most couples endure. I was lucky. Luck-*eee*.

"It's a great deal," Cindy urged in a singsongy voice.

I looked at the price tag and wavered at the sight of the red slash through the original price of $2000 and replaced with the hastily-scrawled $249. I loved red slashes. It's a great deal. And I probably *could* turn around and sell the dress on eBay for a profit. In fact, I might make enough to surprise Barry with plane tickets for a vacation. He'd been wanting to go to Vegas, and I'd been resistant, for reasons that now seem childish...

As childish as me standing here obsessing about buying a gown simply because it resurrected too many memories...? Memories a wedding dress might exorcise...?

"Okay," I said impulsively. "I'll take it."

Cindy clapped her hands, then stopped, as if she

were afraid that her celebrating would change my mind, and herded me toward the checkout counter.

Only later, when a gushing salesclerk handed me the gown, bagged and paid for, was I seized by a sudden, unnerving thought:

What if Cindy's "self-fulfilling prophecy" experiment rubbed off on *me?*

2

THE WHOLE "self-fulfilling prophecy" thing was still nagging at me when I got home and I realized I would have to get rid of something in order to make room for my impulsive purchase. Buyer's remorse struck me hard and I cursed my weakness for a good buy. To punish myself, I laid out the brown suede fringed coat I had splurged on last spring but rarely wore, plus a pair of rivet-studded jeans and a white embroidered shirt that had seemed exotic in the store, but smacked of a costume when I stood before the full-length mirror in my bathroom. I had never worked up the nerve to wear the outfit. As much as I loved the pieces, it seemed unlikely that the urban Western look was going to come back in style anytime soon, and if it did, I obviously couldn't carry it off. But my friend Kenzie could, and since she now lived part-time on a farm in upstate New York, she would probably find a way to wear them and look smashing.

Looking for other things that Kenzie might wear, I unearthed a sweater with running horses on it that

Redford had given me and, after a moment of sentimental indecision, added it to the giveaway bag, as well. Then I hung the wedding gown in the front of the closet because it was the only place the skirt could hang unimpeded by bulging shoe racks.

The phone rang, and I snatched up the handset, wondering who it could be on Saturday afternoon. (I was too cheap to pay for caller ID on my landline phone.) "Hello."

"Hey," Barry said, his voice low and casual. "What are you doing?"

I dropped onto my queen-size bed whose headboard still smelled faintly of woodsmoke two years after the fire sale at which I'd bought it. "Just cleaning out my closet."

"I have good news," he said in a way that made me think that if I'd said, "I just bought a wedding gown," he wouldn't even have noticed.

I worked my mouth from side to side. "What?"

"I just passed Ellen in the hall—you really bowled her over at lunch yesterday."

I sat up, interested. Barry was a producer for one of New York City's local TV stations, and Ellen Brant was the station manager. Barry had referred her to me for financial advice on her divorce. Over lunch I had listened while she had told me the entire sordid story about her cheating husband, while she downed four eighteen-dollar martinis. "But he was a rich sonofabitch," she'd slurred. "And now I have an effing—" (I'm paraphrasing) "—boatload of money to invest."

When she'd told me the amount of money she was talking about, it was more like an effing *yacht*-load (although at the end of the evening she hadn't made a move to pay the slightly obscene bar bill). Grey Goose vodka had bowled her over. I honestly didn't think she'd remember my name…or even my sex, for that matter.

I wet my lips carefully, trying to keep my excitement at bay. "Do you think she'll open an account at Trayser Brothers?"

"I'm almost sure of it. You're still coming to the honors dinner tonight, aren't you?"

"Of course I am. I wouldn't miss seeing you get your award."

"I might not win," he chided.

I *pshawed*, supportive girlfriend that I was.

"Ellen will be there. I'll try to pull her aside and feel her out," he promised.

I was flattered—Barry had never been keenly interested in my profession, but then most people were vaguely suspicious of investment-types, as if we hoarded all the moneymaking secrets for ourselves, while collectively laughing at everyone who trusted us. (Not true—I was currently poor and working toward precisely what I advised all my clients to do: buy your apartment sooner rather than later.) But, Ellen's boatload of money notwithstanding, I felt obligated to point out the potential pitfalls of advising my boyfriend's boss on financial matters. "Barry, you know I appreciate the referral, but…"

"But what?"

"Well, Ellen *is* your boss. I don't want this to be a conflict of interest for you."

He gave a little laugh. "Gee, Denise, it's not as if you and I are married."

Ouch. I glanced at the wedding gown, barely contained by the closet, and my face flamed. "I know, but we're…involved."

"Trust me—it won't be an issue. In fact, Ellen will be indebted to me for introducing her to you. This could turn out great for both of us."

"Okay," I said cheerfully, pushing aside my reservations.

So help me, dollar signs were dancing behind my eyelids. I could picture the look on old Mr. Trayser's face when I announced in the Monday morning staff meeting that I'd just landed an eight-figure account. "Partner" didn't seem as far-fetched as it had last week…or at least an office with a window.

"What's the dress code for this evening?"

He made a rueful noise. "Dressy. And Ellen is a bit of a clotheshorse. I'm not saying it'll make a difference…"

"But it might," I finished, my cheeks warming when I remembered the woman's critical glance over my aged navy suit and serviceable pumps yesterday. I wasn't exactly famous for my style—my *most* trendy clothes were season-old steals from designer outlets. I was more of an off-the-rack kind of girl, and I didn't relish running up my credit card for a one-night outfit. But drastic times called for plastic measures. "I'll find something nice," I promised.

"I know you'll make me look good."

I blinked—Barry considered me a reflection on him? That was serious couple-stuff...wasn't it? I straightened with pride at his compliment.

"I'll pick you up at seven."

"Great," I said. "Oh, and thanks...Barry...for the recommendation." We had never quite graduated to pet names and as tempted as I was to say "sweetie" or "hon," I decided that while he was hooking me up with a revenue stream with his boss, this might not be the best time to start getting gushy.

"Anything for you," he said, then hung up.

I smiled, but when I disconnected the phone, panic immediately set in—I had two pimples from last week's peanut M&M's binge, and my nails were a wreck. It would be next to impossible to get a manicure at the last minute on Saturday.

I jumped up and whirled into action. After a shower, I dialed the cell phone of my friend Kenzie Mansfield Long, who was the most stylish person I knew; although I wasn't sure if she'd have service in the rural area of the state where she lived on weekends.

"Hello?" she sang into the receiver.

"Hi, it's Denise. I was taking a chance on reaching you—you have service now?"

"A tower just went up on the next ridge. Jar Hollow officially has cellular service."

"Did Sam arrange that just for you?" I asked with

a laugh. Her doting veterinarian husband was doing everything in his power to make country living more bearable for his city-bred wife, à la Lisa in *Green Acres.*

"The service isn't just for me," Kenzie protested. "It's for the entire town. And it helps me and Sam to stay in touch when we're apart during the week."

At the mischievous note in my friend's voice, I had the feeling that phone sex supplemented the couple's seemingly insatiable lust for each other. Kenzie's— or should I say *Sam's*—homemade dildo cast from the real, um, *thing* was infamous among our circle of friends. After seeing it, I could barely make eye contact with the man. In fact, it was that darn dildo that had resurrected my fantasies of Redford. He had been an amazing specimen of virility and, um…dimension.

Okay, the man was hung like a stallion…not that I'd ever seen a stallion's penis, but word on the street was that the equine species was gifted in that department. The fact that Redford's family in Kentucky was in the horse business had burned the association even deeper into my depraved brain.

No, I wasn't jealous of Kenzie's relationship with Sam…most of the time. I had known great, mind-blowing lust with Redford, but our relationship had burned out as quickly as a cheap candle. Barry, on the other hand, was no dynamo in bed, but he had staying power in other areas.

His IRA account was a whopper.

"How was the 'running of the brides'?" Kenzie

asked, breaking into my strange musings. "Did Cindy find a gown?"

"Yes," I said, then decided to 'fess up before Cindy told on me. "And I, um, bought a gown, too."

There was silence on the other end, then, "Barry *proposed?*"

"No," I said quickly, feeling like an idiot. "But I thought, you know, if ever….well…the dress was dirt cheap," I finished lamely.

"Ah," Kenzie said. "A bargain—now I understand. Well, one of these days, Barry is bound to come around. Valentine's Day is just around the corner, you know."

"Subject change. I called because I have a style emergency." I explained about the honors dinner and my desire to wow Ellen Brant and her pocketbook with my stunning sense of fashion. "Any suggestions?"

"You could wear your wedding gown," Kenzie said, then cracked up laughing.

"I'm hanging up."

"I'm *kidding*. Gee, lighten up." Then she snapped her fingers. "I saw the cutest striped dress in the window of Benderlee's, and I remember thinking it would look smashing on you."

"Will it smash the credit line on my VISA card?"

"Probably, but think of it as an investment." She laughed. "Knowing you, you'll think of a way to write the dress off on your taxes as a business expense."

"Ha, ha."

"I'm not kidding— I can't believe how much Sam

and I are getting back on our taxes this year, thanks to you. If you ever decide to go into tax preparation, I want to invest."

I laughed. "Thanks."

"And go to Nordstrom's for shoes. Ask for Lito, tell him I sent you."

My shoulders fell. "Okay."

"And tell me you're not going to wear your hair in a ponytail."

I squinted. "I'm not going to wear my hair in a ponytail?"

"For goodness' sake, Denise, loosen up. Your ponytail is so tight, it's a wonder you don't have an aneurysm."

My friends were good at reminding me that I was a tight ass. And a tight*wad*. "I'm loose," I argued, rolling my shoulders in my best imitation of a "groove"—until my neck popped painfully. I grimaced—was it possible to break your own neck?

"Wear your hair down and buy a pair of chandelier earrings."

"You think?"

"I was under the impression that you called for my advice."

"I did."

"You want this woman's business, don't you?"

"Yes."

"Then you gotta do what you gotta do."

I sighed. "You're right."

"So…Barry set you up to do business with his

boss," she said in a singsongy tone. "Maybe it's a good thing you bought that wedding gown. It sounds like he's thinking long-term."

I glanced at the dress I had so foolishly purchased and gave a nervous little laugh. "Or maybe he's trying to suck up to his boss."

"Hmm. Sounds like someone needs to take a lesson from Cindy in positive thinking."

I thanked Kenzie for her help, then hung up with a cleansing exhale. Kenzie was right—I should be grateful for the opportunity that Barry had made for me, instead of questioning his motives. I was letting my frustration with our lackluster sex life color other aspects of our relationship. It was embarrassing, really—I was an intelligent woman. I had proof that elements other than sex were more important to a successful long-term, um…association. Financial compatibility, for instance. Sex waned over time. But dividend reinvestment stock plans were forever.

A sudden thought prompted me to pick up the phone and order two plane tickets to Las Vegas for a long weekend as a Valentine's Day surprise for Barry. When I hung up, I heaved a sigh, feeling much better. Then I slanted a frown toward my bedroom.

I was suffering from a bad case of the all-overs, and the culprit was taking up too much room in my closet. I was already letting that ridiculous wedding gown interfere with our relationship, and for no good reason. Barry needn't ever know what I'd done. Tomorrow I'd put that sucker on eBay and be rid of it for good.

Er—the dress, not Barry.

3

KENZIE WAS RIGHT—the dress in Benderlee's window looked better on me than the average frock, so I bought it despite the breathtaking price. And Lito at Nordstrom's had hooked me up with a pair of shoes with an equally stunning price tag. If I wore them every day for the rest of my life, I might get my money's worth out of them. Throwing caution to the wind, I had also bought a chic gray wool coat. I left my hair long and loose, which made me feel a little unkempt, but I have to admit I was feeling rather spiffy when Barry arrived. I opened the door with a coy smile.

He looked polished and professional in a navy suit, striped tie, not a pale blond hair out of place. "Ready to go?" he asked, then pointed to his watch. "Traffic is a nightmare."

My smile slipped. "I...yes."

"Good, because I'd hate to be late."

Barry wasn't the most attentive man I'd ever known, but tonight he seemed unusually preoccupied. Then I realized he was probably more anxious about the award for which he'd been nominated than he wanted to let on. Indeed, on the drive to the hotel, he checked his watch at least a hundred times, his expression pinched. And he seemed to be coming down with a cold since he sneezed several times. To see my normally calm, collected boyfriend so fidgety moved me. I reached over to squeeze his hand. "Relax. I hope you have a thank-you speech prepared."

He smiled sheepishly. "I made a few notes...just in case."

I instantly forgave him for not noticing how fabulous I looked. Besides, I reminded myself, I had dressed for Ellen Brant, and as luck would have it, we were seated at her table for the awards ceremony. In fact, by some bizarre shuffling of bodies and chairs, she wound up sitting between us. The woman was so cosmopolitan, even in my new clothes I felt gauche. I raised my finger for a nervous nibble on my nail, and tasted the bitter tang of fresh nail polish...a do-it-myself manicure was the best I could manage under the circumstances.

"Denise, your dress is divine," she murmured over her martini glass.

"Thank you," I said, taking my finger out of my mouth and sitting up straighter.

"She's smart *and* fashionable," Ellen said to Barry for my benefit. "I like this girl."

"She's dependable, too," Barry said. "And loyal."

I managed to conceal my surprise at his bizarre statement. Until I realized that to Ellen, recently betrayed by her husband, loyalty was essential. So on cue, I nodded like a puppy dog.

Ellen pursed her collagen-plumped lips. "Denise, why don't you call me next week and we'll go over the paperwork for that investment account."

"Okay," I said in a voice that belied my excitement. If Ellen opened an account at Trayser Brothers, I'd be able to pay off my outfit *and* buy my apartment. Plus a new bed that didn't reek of woodsmoke. A closet organization system. Caller ID.

I could scarcely eat I was so wound up. I tried to contribute to the conversation, but Ellen and Barry were soon absorbed in television-speak, and I thought it best not to intrude. Barry was, after all, hoping for a promotion, and Ellen would drive that decision. Instead, I chatted with other people seated at the table, spurred to a higher degree of socialization than usual by the open bar. Happily, the evening was topped off by a slightly tipsy Ellen presenting Barry with the award for excellence in producing that was acknowledged in the industry as a precursor to the Emmy.

For his part, Barry was the most excited I'd ever seen him—which was no compliment to me, I realized suddenly. But I postponed an untimely (and uncomfortable) analysis of our love life by clapping wildly. I told myself it was okay that he didn't name me personally in his thank-you speech, a fact that he seemed truly distressed over later when we were in the car.

"I forgot my notes and I went completely blank," he said in the semi-darkness, his hands on the steering wheel at the ten and two positions—he was a fastidious driver. "I'm sorry, Denise. You're the one who's had to put up with my long hours and my traveling."

"It's fine," I murmured. "I'm just so proud of you. And I know Ellen is impressed."

He made a dismissive noise, but was clearly pleased. Then he winced. "Oh, by the way, Ellen asked me tonight to be in L.A. Monday morning."

My good mood wedged in my throat. His travel to the West Coast had become more frequent in the past couple of months—in the wee hours of the morning, I wondered if something other than work drew him there. After all, if I wasn't thrilled with our sex life, he probably wasn't, either. "How long will you be gone?"

"Two weeks, maybe three."

"That's almost a month," I said, hating the way I sounded—horny.

"No, it isn't," he said with a practicality that did not put me at ease.

"You'll miss Valentine's Day."

He looked apologetic. "I'm sorry, Denise. Right now I have to focus on this promotion. I'll make it up to you, I promise."

"Want to spend the night?" I asked, not caring that I was being transparent.

He looked over at me and laughed. "Sure."

I smiled all the way home, determined that tonight

Barry and I would have great, boisterous sex. I might even pull out some of the tricks that Redford had taught me that I'd never shared with anyone else. I had shaved my legs to get ready for the dinner, so nothing was holding me back.

Unfortunately, we drove straight into a traffic jam in midtown that left us in gridlock. After thirty minutes had passed with no movement, I began to dwell on Barry's comment that I was dependable…and loyal. He made me sound like a cocker spaniel.

I studied his profile, noting how preoccupied he was, and realized abruptly that we had fallen into a serious rut. No wonder we'd never talked about marriage—we rarely saw each other and we rarely had sex.

For all intents and purposes, we were *already* married.

Feeling rebellious, I ran my fingers through my loose hair and whispered, "We could have sex right here."

Barry looked over at me with a shocked expression, then laughed nervously and gestured to the cars around his silver Lexus. "Are you crazy? We'd be arrested for indecent exposure. A stunt like that would mean my job, Denise."

I pulled back, humiliated at my own behavior. He was right, of course. The network's top female anchor had gone out drinking one night and performed a topless dance at a bar where at least one handheld video camera had been rolling, and everyone had been put on notice. Barry couldn't jeopardize his job just because I was feeling neglected. So we listened to National Public Radio and chatted about the evening.

"You seemed to be having a good time talking to everyone," Barry said. "Everyone thought you were great. Everyone loves you, Denise."

Something in his voice made me turn my head to look at him in the semi-darkness. He'd spoken with a sort of wistfulness when he'd said "everyone loves you," as if everyone else saw something he didn't. I waited for clarification, but Barry simply scanned the traffic, tapping his finger on the steering wheel to a jazzy song floating from the speakers.

I was imagining things. Barry loved me. He hadn't changed—I had. More specifically, that stupid wedding dress had made me paranoid.

And reflective.

Because the wedding dress had made me confront the possibility of marrying Barry…was it something I wanted? And if not, then what was the purpose of our being together? Companionship? An occasional sexual release? Were we merely a pit stop for each other on the way to…something else? I was suddenly seized by the feeling that I was looking at someone I'd known for years. Yet…did I really know him?

In hindsight, I'd known little about Redford when I'd married him—beyond his sexual prowess. A sudden stab of desire struck my midsection, but I closed my eyes against it.

During those few days with Redford in Las Vegas, I had been a different person, wanton and hedonistic…a bona fide nymphomaniac. I don't know what had come over me…okay, admittedly, *Redford* had come over me a few times, but I digress. My parents—especially my mother—would be appalled if they knew how I had behaved during that time, and my girlfriends would be shocked. I could scarcely think of it myself without being overcome with shame—nice girls didn't do the things I'd done with Redford. Especially after knowing the man for mere hours.

At the time, I'd thought that Redford DeMoss, with his chiseled good looks, military manners and tantric sex sessions was the most exotic creature I'd ever encountered. I'd only dated city boys who were competitive and frenzied. Redford's easy confidence and sexual aura had literally knocked me off my feet. Only later, after I'd returned to New York, did I admit to myself that everything that came out of his sensual mouth—words about down-home cookin', home-grown lovin' and small-town livin'—came straight out of a country song. He'd been playing a part—hell, we both had. It was a love-at-first-sight fantasy. We'd had no business getting married.

"Denise?"

I blinked myself back to the present and stared at Barry, who was staring at me. "Huh?"

He frowned and rubbed one of his eyes. "I asked if I left any of my allergy medicine at your place. If not, maybe we should backtrack to my apartment."

While I had been winding down memory lane, the traffic had begun to unravel. I was suddenly eager to get home—to my cozy apartment, not to Barry's sterile condo. "You left your toiletry bag at my place when you came back from L.A. Are your allergies acting up?"

"Yeah," he said, nodding toward my new coat. "I think it's the wool."

"Oh. Sorry."

"No problem," he said. "By the way, I noticed your new outfit. Good job."

"Thank you," I said, unsure whether or not he'd just paid me a compliment.

He squinted in my direction. "Did you cut your hair?"

"Um, no…I left it down."

"Oh. It looks…mussed. It's a different look for you."

I laughed. "I guess you'll feel like you're making love to a different woman tonight."

"Yeah." Except *he* didn't laugh.

While I pondered my state of mind and general mental health, Barry's cell phone rang—a crisis at the station—and he remained on the call through parking the car near my apartment, the walk thereto, and the walk therein, rubbing his watery eyes intermittently. Still talking, he headed for the bathroom, presumably in search of his allergy medicine. I scooped up the mail that had been pushed through the door slot and tossed it on the end table, then went to the kitchen to fix coffee for endurance (I was still feeling optimistic).

Listening to the distant murmur of Barry's voice,

I watched the coffee drip and gave myself a stern pep talk (no fantasizing about other men—i.e., Redford—while making love this time), and, to my credit, I'd managed to work up a pretty good lust by the time I carried a tray with two cups of coffee to the bedroom.

Not that it mattered. Barry lay sprawled across the bed, fully dressed except for his shoes, his cell phone closed in his limp hand. His toiletry bag lay open next to him—the allergy medicine had apparently kicked in rather quickly. I retraced my steps to the living room and drowned my disappointment in my coffee, which was a mistake, since it left me wide awake.

I found a grainy old movie on television and settled back with a cushion across my stomach. But my mind, as it is wont to do in the wee hours, spun into isolated corners of my psyche, stirring up depressing questions. Was Barry *the one,* or was I simply pinning all my expectations on him and our sexual friendship? Was my soul mate still out there somewhere, waiting for me to materialize? And the most depressing question of all: What if Redford DeMoss had been my one true love?

I brought the cushion to my face and exhaled into it. I knew I had hit rock-bottom lonely when I started thinking about Redford. He was a brief, distant episode in my life…a mistake. The speedy annulment only spared us both more grief and circumvented the inevitable split when he returned from the Gulf. And for me, it helped to gloss over the humiliation of having married someone like Redford. We were such polar opposites, and a quickie marriage in Las Vegas was so, *so* unlike me. At hearing the news, my friends had been, in a word, stunned. No—*flabbergasted* would be a more apt description. And my sweet, loving parents who lived in Florida…well, I'd never quite gotten around to telling them.

Similarly, there had never been a good time to tell Barry.

My face burned just thinking about it…and Redford. He had been insatiable in bed, with the endurance of a marathoner. I cast a glance toward the bedroom where the sound of Barry's soft snores escaped, and felt a pang of guilt. It wasn't fair to him that I compared the two of them in that regard. Redford had been on leave from the Gulf—he probably would've humped a picket fence. Although if we hadn't bumped into each other, he would've had no problem finding another willing partner. A compelling figure in his dress blues, Redford had oozed sex appeal—in and out of uniform. I closed my eyes, recalling my first memory of him.

I had been standing in line to check in to the Paradisio hotel in Vegas, fretting over Cindy's late arrival, when a tall, lone officer had walked in. He must have drawn all the energy from the room, because I remember suddenly having trouble breathing. The manager had offered him expedited service to circumvent the long line, but Redford had refused special treatment. I couldn't take my eyes off him—his broad shoulders had filled the uniform jacket, his posture proud, but his expression relaxed and friendly. My body had vibrated as if I'd been strummed, every cell had strained toward him. He'd caught me looking and winked. Mortified at my uncharacteristic behavior, I'd looked away. But later, we had found each other again.

And again…and again…and again…

I gave myself a shake to dispel my destructive train of thought. Great sex did not a relationship make—as evidenced by my short-lived marriage.

Forcing my mind elsewhere, I picked up my mail from the end table, hoping the caffeine would wear off soon.

There were lots of credit card offers, which I immediately ripped into small pieces, just as I advised my clients to do. There was an appointment reminder from my OB/GYN for a few weeks from now—yippee. There were bills, of course, and several useless catalogs. There was a thank-you note from Kenzie and Sam for a gift I'd sent for their log cabin in upstate New York. A postcard from my folks from their seniors' tour in England—they were having a good time, although Dad missed cold beer. And there was a long manila envelope—I squinted—from the Internal Revenue Service?

I studied the address: Mr. and Mrs. Redford De-Moss. My heart lurched crazily, followed by relief. This was obviously some sort of mistake. Redford and I had filed taxes once because our abbreviated marriage had spanned the end of a calendar year. I had filled out the forms myself because I'd wanted to make sure they were done properly (and economically).

Still, my hands were unsteady as I tore open the envelope, and slid out the letter written on heavy bonded paper. I skimmed the words, barely seeing the print. I was familiar with the form letter—in my line of work as a financial planner, I'd seen this same letter dozens of times, only not directed toward *me*.

Redford and I, it seemed, were being audited.

4

FOR AN HOUR I WAS NUMB. Alternately I stared at and reread the IRS letter commanding me and Redford to appear ten days hence, bearing proof that the joint return we'd filed three years ago was accurate as it pertained to a couple of items—primarily our income and the deductions we'd taken.

Or rather, the deductions *I* had taken. It had been the time frame when I was getting my financial planning business off the ground and, admittedly, I had taken some rather aggressive deductions regarding a home office. I chewed one home-manicured fingernail to the quick, then began to gnaw on a second. The fact that I was being audited by the IRS would not be perceived as a plus by my employer, or among my clients and potential clients. Ellen Brant, for instance, wouldn't take kindly to the news. Barry—

My heart skipped a beat or two or three. Oh, God, *what* was I going to tell Barry about Redford?

Barry, there's a tiny detail about my past I keep forgetting to mention...

Barry, you're not going to believe this...

Barry, want to hear something funny?

Nausea rolled in my stomach. I couldn't tell him about my annulled marriage *now*—he'd think I was only telling him because I had to.

Which was true, but still...

No, I'd have to be careful to keep this audit business under wraps. I paced and hummed to keep the panic at bay, my mind racing for a way out of the mess I'd landed in.

Suddenly I brightened: Barry would be in L.A. for two, maybe three weeks. By the time he returned to New York, the situation with Redford would be put to bed—er, put to *rest*.

If I were very, very careful, I'd come out of this situation unscathed.

I rubbed my roiling stomach. As if the secrecy and the possibility of being slapped with a fine or a penalty wasn't enough to give me a bleeding ulcer, there was the thought of being reunited with Redford.

Would he come to Manhattan? Then I scoffed—of course he'd come if he were Stateside. Under order of the IRS, he *had* to come. Probably with a new, young wife in tow, and maybe even a kidlet or two. They'd make it a family vacation—see the Met, the Statue of Liberty, the ex-wife.

Although, in truth, I wasn't really his ex-wife because the annulment meant I'd never *been* his wife. The potential complications swirled in my head, overridden by one gut-clenching question—had Redford thought about me since our annulment?

Annulment. Our marriage had been such an egregious mistake, it had to be indelibly erased. I eased onto the edge of a straight-back chair, remembering how overwhelmed I'd felt when I'd filed those papers. When I'd first arrived back in New York, I had still been awash with my lust for Redford, wistful and optimistic and certain we'd be able to work through any obstacles to be together. He would visit me in New York when he had leave from the Gulf and when he returned to his station in North Carolina. Then I would join him on his family horse farm in Kentucky when he retired from the Marine Corps in a couple of years. With his vision and my financial know-how, we'd grow the business exponentially. He'd made everything seem so…possible. I had been buoyed by the light of adventure in his eyes and blinded by the promises in his lovemaking.

But doubts about our relationship had set in almost immediately. I'd felt isolated and alone. He had warned me it might be weeks before he could call me or e-mail, and since none of my girlfriends had been with me in Vegas, I had no one to reassure me that I hadn't imagined my and Redford's feelings toward each other. Indeed, when I'd announced I'd gotten married, they all thought I was joking—sensible, down-to-earth Denise would never marry a virtual stranger in Vegas. Had I gone completely mad?

I didn't even *like* horses.

When I started thinking about how little I knew about Redford and how much longer he would be in the Marines, my doubts had snowballed. His comment about not being able to communicate with me had seemed lame. But it was the article that appeared in the newspaper a few days later that had pushed me over the edge: G.I.'s Desperate To Say "I Do."

I would never forget that headline. The story went on to describe how soldiers on leave from the Middle East conflict were driven to marry the first willing girl they met because they were afraid they wouldn't come home, and eager to have someone waiting for them if they did. Not surprising, the story went on to say, the divorce and annulment rates for those speedy marriages were astronomical. The women were portrayed as desperate in their own right—caught up in their desire to attach themselves to an alpha male out of social loyalty and the pursuit of cinematic romanticism.

Cinematic romanticism. According to the article, I wasn't in love with Redford—I was in love with the *idea* of Redford. Which explained why I would have fallen for someone who was so polar opposite to me, so radically different from the "type" of guy I usually dated…and so quickly. Over the next few days, I had come to the conclusion that it all had been a big, honking mistake. As soon as I'd gotten my period (thank you, God), I'd settled on an annulment.

Through the Internet I'd found a Vegas attorney to file the petition for a civil annulment. He'd had a greasy demeanor that made me feel soiled, but he seemed to be experienced in dissolving quickie marriages. He'd filed the petition on the grounds that "before entering into the marriage, the plaintiff and defendant did not know each other's likes and dislikes, each other's desires to have or not have children and each other's desires as to state of residency."

All true, except for the part about having children. Redford had expressed a desire for little ones, girls in particular. But I had assuaged my guilt by the fact that we hadn't discussed when or how many.

The attorney warned me that Redford could contest the annulment, and I have to admit that a small part of me had hoped he would. But upon returning to his unit, he must have come to some of the same conclusions because the papers were returned promptly, with his signature scrawled across the bottom, making it official: Redford and I had never been man and wife. Kenzie, Cindy and Jacki pledged their secrecy, and I pledged to drive Redford from my mind. They had kept their pledge. I had been somewhat more lax.

Sometimes a month would go by without me thinking of him. And then something out of the blue would trigger a repressed memory and I would spend a sweat-soaked night reliving the amazing ways Redford had turned my body inside out…the ways he had stroked and plied me to pleasure heights I hadn't known existed. Then whispered that he loved me and had taken me higher still.

During those long, lonely hours, regrets would hit me hard. I'd close my eyes against the dark and fantasize about still having Redford in my bed, with his strong arms and legs wrapped around me, his warm sex inside of me, his sigh in my ear. And I would entertain what-ifs…

The mornings after those tortuous nights I would drag my sleep-ravaged body out of my cold bed and promise myself it would be the last time I would lose sleep over Redford DeMoss. I attributed my recent and more frequent recollections of him to all the weddings and bridal talk among my friends—I had consoled myself that the wayward thoughts would recede when the excitement passed.

But now I wondered crazily if I had somehow willed this IRS audit through all the kinetic vibes about Redford that I had sent out into the universe. Cindy's theory about a self-fulfilling prophecy taunted me…

I don't remember falling asleep. One minute I was stewing in troubling memories, and the next, Barry was shaking me awake and sunshine streamed in the windows.

"Why did you sleep on the couch?" he asked, his eyebrows knitted.

"I was watching a movie," I mumbled, pointing to the TV, which was still on. I felt thoroughly miserable, still wearing my expensive (and now crumpled) dress, my face gummy with old makeup, my mouth furry and hot. At the crackle of the IRS letter beneath my hip, panic struck me anew.

Thankfully, Barry didn't notice the letter. He

reached toward me and pushed my hair out of my eyes, gazing at me with concern. "Are you all right?"

"Sure," I lied.

"Are *we* all right?" he asked, surprising me.

But it was just the gentle reminder I needed to bring me back to the present. Barry was here and he cared. My heart squeezed and I nodded. "Of course we are."

He smiled, seemingly relieved. "You know I love you."

I blinked. Barry and I had professed our affection for each other before, but he wasn't particularly verbal about his feelings. "I know," I murmured, feeling guilty that only last night I had questioned his loyalty to me.

"Good," he said. "I'm sorry about zonking out on you last night. I guess I was more tired than I realized, and the allergy medication took care of the rest."

"That's okay."

"So," he said, his voice suddenly sultry, "how about letting me make it up to you tonight—meet me at Millweed's at seven?"

My eyes widened. "A girl can't say no to Millweed's."

He winked and kissed my ear. "My thoughts exactly. I need to take off." He stood and pulled on the jacket he'd been wearing last night, then picked up his toiletry bag and moved toward the door. "Do you have any big plans today?"

Track down my ex-husband. I swallowed and con-

sidered telling Barry about the letter that was burning into my thigh. But I didn't want to break the romantic mood or raise any red flags. Besides, who
knew if I would even be able to locate Redford? If
he were still overseas, the audit would be a moot
point. It seemed silly to bring up the subject in the
event it amounted to nothing.

"No big plans," I said breezily.

"Okay, see you later."

My heart moved guiltily. "Wait," I called, and
sprang up from the couch, heedless of where the letter might fall. I ran over to the door to stretch up and
give Barry a full-body hug. "See you later."

He grinned, then angled his head. "You have
something stuck to your butt." Before I could react,
he reached around and peeled the letter from my
backside.

I snatched it out of his hand and manufactured
a laugh. "It's nothing," I said, crumpling the letter.
"Junk mail," I added for convincing detail. Then I
shooed him out the door and closed it more forcefully
than I intended.

Sighing in relief, I leaned against the door and
smoothed out the letter, just in case its meaning was
somehow less ominous in the light of day.

I scanned the words addressed to Mr. and Mrs.
Redford DeMoss and worked my mouth from side to
side. No—just as ominous. A slow drip of panic
started to raise the acid level in my stomach. How
could I prepare myself for speaking to Redford again?

Assuming I could track him down, would he be angry? Belligerent? Aloof? Sarcastic? Disinterested?

Mrs. Redford DeMoss. Denise DeMoss. Redford had said it sounded like a movie star's name, and that I was as beautiful as one...

I set aside the letter long enough to take a shower. But as soon as I closed my eyes to allow the warm water to run over my face and shoulders, memories of Redford came flooding back. Everything about the man had been big—his body, his laugh, his spirit. He had made me feel special and protected and desirable. His lovemaking had awakened a dark, daring side of me that I hadn't known I possessed. He had been a generous lover—slow, thorough and innovative. I was pretty sure that a few of the things we had done were illegal in some states.

With a start, I realized my body had started to respond to the erotic memories. Feeling sentimental and keenly frustrated from my lack of sex, I slid my hands down my stomach to lather the curls at the juncture of my thighs, thrilling from the warmth of the water and the slick pressure of my soapy fingers. Redford had adored making love in the shower, had kissed and suckled and caressed me until I nearly drowned. He had an amazing way of prepping my body with his fingers, readying me for his entry until I thought I would die from wanting him inside me. My own fingers weren't as strong and firm, but they found the essence of my pleasure ably enough, and strangely, even though there were some details about

Redford that had faded in my mind, when I closed my eyes and sent my mind and body back in time, I could conjure up his presence in two breaths.

I leaned into the tiled wall and he leaned into me, the shower spray bouncing off his broad, muscled shoulders, his dark hair slicked back from his tanned face, his sensuous mouth nuzzling my shoulder, the soapy water mingling on our skin. He seemed to derive pleasure from mine, pleased that he could excite me, murmuring encouragement and throaty laughs when I was close to climaxing.

"I want to hear you, Denise...tell me how good it feels..."

I'd never been with anyone who was so...*conversational* during sex. The novelty of it—and the naughtiness—had pushed my level of sensitivity higher than I'd thought possible. "Um...oh...Redford...it feels wonderful...feels like...I'm going to...explode."

And I did, convulsing as the warm water pulsed over me, losing myself in the exquisite torture of a powerful orgasm that weakened my knees. I slid down the wall and sat on the shower floor, shuddering, recovering slowly under the cooling spray. As always, the inevitable guilt set in.

I told myself that I had fantasized about Redford this time only because Barry had left me in a state of unfulfilled arousal. And Redford was uppermost in my mind only because of the IRS letter. I was a sensible woman—everyone said so. What possible good could come of rehashing the past?

I turned off the shower, stepped out and pulled on a robe, giving myself a mental shake. But my traitorous feet took me into the bedroom to stand in front of the trunk at the foot of my bed, and I relented with a sigh. My heart was clicking as I raised the lid and moved aside family photo albums, high school and college yearbooks, and a box of cards and letters I'd collected over the years, my fingers keen to find a secret cache.

At the bottom of the trunk in a corner sat a Punch cigar box—the brand that Redford had smoked. I'd never before dated a man who smoked cigars; I remembered finding it so male and strangely attractive. Over the past couple of years I had felt comforted by the fact that I couldn't conjure up a picture of Redford in my mind—it convinced me that what I'd felt for him was a mirage. But when I touched the smooth surface of the box, I could clearly see him smiling and smoking a cigar by the pool at the Las Vegas hotel where we'd stayed.

Thick, dark hair with sun-lightened streaks, bronzed skin, laughing black eyes, sharp cheekbones...and a Tom Cruise smile that made me want to sprawl on the nearest horizontal surface in hopes he would trip and fall on me.

He had fallen on me quite a lot—that detail was burned into my memory.

My hand shook as I removed the cigar box, untouched since I'd left it there just over three years ago. When I lifted the lid, my breath caught in my throat and I felt as if I was being pulled backward through a time tunnel.

The gray velvet box holding my wedding ring sat on top. I used two hands to open it and at the sight of the wide gold filigree band, I was overcome with bittersweet memories…

"Do you like it?" Redford had asked while we were standing in the most garish jewelry store in the western hemisphere. Among the flashing lights and salesmen with bullhorns, I'd been doubtful we could find anything simple. But Redford had pulled one of the salesmen aside and cajoled the man into showing him the estate jewelry that Redford was sure was being held in the back for special customers. Sure enough, the man had disappeared, then returned with a tray of exquisite rings. I had fallen in love with the filigree band on sight…much like I had with Redford.

As I gazed at the ring, bittersweet pangs struck my chest. I was mistaken about being in love with Redford, but I was still in love with the gorgeous wedding band. He had paid an enormous sum for it—we'd argued over the cost, but Redford had parted with his money during our time together as if there were no tomorrow. And according to the newspaper article, that had been Redford's frame of mind exactly.

I had sent the ring to the attorney to include with the annulment papers that were served to Redford, but Redford had returned the ring with the signed papers with no explanation. The attorney had advised me to sell the ring to offset the fees of the annulment, but I couldn't bring myself to do it at the time…or since.

I bit my lip and snapped the ring box closed, then set it aside to riffle through the remaining contents of the cigar box: a coaster from the hotel bar, a matchbook from the place he'd taken me dancing, the key to our room at the Paradisio hotel, ticket stubs to shows, a party horn, postcards, our marriage license, the annulment papers, and our wedding pictures.

I knew women who had hired no fewer than three photographers on the day of their wedding to circumvent a no-show, faulty equipment, or a drunk cameraman. Other women had white satin albums trimmed with ribbon and lace, crammed with studio-quality photos of them in their designer gown, a glowing groom, twelve bridesmaids, twelve groomsmen, three flower girls and a ring bearer. Other women had 5x7s, 8x10s and 16x20s of the special day. I had three blurry Polaroid pictures.

The first showed the two of us smiling at the camera through the driver's-side window of Redford's rental car. In the second picture, I wore a paper veil and held a small bouquet of silk flowers. We were exchanging vows—Redford's mouth was open slightly, caught midword. His voice came floating back to me, a deep, throaty drawl that had wrapped around me and stroked me like a big, vibrating hand…silken sandpaper. A shiver skated over my shoulders—apparently memory cells existed in every part of one's body.

The third picture showed us kissing as man and wife. Unbidden, my mouth tingled and the elusive elements of his kiss came back to me—the way his eyes darkened as he inched closer, the possessive feel of his mouth against mine, the promise of his tongue...

With effort, I forced myself back to the present and to the photo in my hand. We were covered in confetti the witness had tossed on us through the open window. Redford was wearing a black sweatshirt. I couldn't tell from the photo, but remembered that I'd been wearing a T-shirt with no bra, my hair messy and hanging around my shoulders, not a speck of makeup. Natural, hedonistic...what had I been thinking?

In hindsight, I hadn't been thinking—at least not beyond the next orgasm. Redford had been the first man to tap in to my sexuality and I'd been blinded by lust. I had mistaken enthusiasm for love.

I did have a fourth picture, although not of our wedding. I carefully withdrew the framed 5x7 from the box, drinking in the sight of First Sergeant DeMoss in his dress uniform, achingly handsome in his official U.S. Marine Corps photo. He had given it to me somewhat sheepishly at the airport, and I had clutched it all the way back to New York. I ran my finger over his face, my heart full over my naiveté at the time.

The phone rang and I picked up the handset on the nightstand, happy for a diversion from the troubling thoughts on the continuous loop in my head. "Hello?"

"Hey, it's Kenzie."

I smiled into the phone. "Hey, yourself."

"So, did you wow the boss lady last night?"

"The dress was a hit. Thanks again for your help."

"Did you get the account?"

"I'll find out more this week, but I'm hopeful."

"You'll have to call me in Jar Hollow to let me know how it goes."

"You're not coming back to the city this week?"

"No, that's another reason I called— Oh, wait, Sam just walked in and I need to, um…give him a message. Can I call you back?"

"Sure," I said, then hung up with a smirk. A message—right. Good grief, the two of them were like teenagers. But I wasn't jealous…really I wasn't.

I tried not to imagine the acrobatics going on in Jar Hollow while I stared at Redford's picture and waited for Kenzie to call me back. The phone rang again less than two minutes later—of course, if the stories were true, she and Sam had had time for a quickie. I picked up the phone and sighed dramatically. "*Please* stop dangling your sex in front of me."

Dead silence sounded on the line.

My chest blipped with panic. "Hello?"

A deep, rumbling laugh rolled out. "Well, that's what I call picking up where we left off."

I swallowed. "Who...who is this?" But I would have recognized that orgasmic voice anywhere.

5

LAUGHTER BOOMED over the phone again. "It's Redford, Denise—your ex-husband. Who did you think it was?"

I was instantly nervous, hearing his voice when my body still vibrated from his memory-induced orgasm. "Um...someone else."

"Sounds like a pretty interesting conversation," he said, his smooth Southern voice infused with amusement. "If this is a bad time, I can call back."

"No," I blurted, my cheeks flaming. "I can talk now."

"Good," he said easily. "Listen, I got a letter from the IRS yesterday—looks like the government wants a little more of my time."

"I received the same letter," I said, regaining a modicum of composure. "You're out of the Marines?"

"Retired for almost six months now."

"Where do you live?"

"In Kentucky. Versailles, to be exact. This is where the girls are."

So he had children—the girls he'd wanted. I don't know why the news surprised me, but my disappointment was acute. And then I realized that Redford having a family certainly made things easier for me—I could shake my stubborn fantasies once and for all.

"That's nice," I managed.

"And you're still living in the same place?"

In other words, my life hadn't changed a bit. My chin went up. "I'll be buying my apartment soon."

"Great. So, do you live alone?"

I frowned. "Yes."

"No kidding? I thought you'd be remarried by now."

"Um, no, I'm not married." I stared at my closet door—plastic covering the wedding gown stuck out from under the door, mocking me.

"Not married? Don't tell me I ruined you for other men," he teased.

Had he always been so cocky? My mouth tightened. "Not at all."

"Darn. And here I was hoping that you still carried my picture around."

I glanced down at the framed picture still in my hand and dropped it back into the cigar box as if it were on fire. "Sorry to disappoint."

He cleared his throat, as if he realized he'd overstepped his bounds. "Well, Denise, what do you know about this audit?"

"No more than what the letter said."

"Three years seems like a long time to have lapsed to be audited." He sounded concerned.

"No," I assured him. "Considering the backlog at the IRS, I'd say three years is about right."

"Are you still a financial planner?"

"Yes. I work for a brokerage firm now."

"Congratulations. Does that give us an advantage? I mean, do you deal with the IRS often?"

"Only as an advisor to my clients regarding payment of fees or penalties."

At the sudden silence on the other end, I realized my response wasn't exactly comforting, and since the audit was most likely a result of my creative accounting, I felt as if I owed him a little reassurance.

"Redford, chances are this will be a routine interview. They'll probably just want to ask us a few questions, see a few receipts, that sort of thing."

He gave a little laugh. "I don't even know where my tax records are—in storage somewhere."

"I kept everything," I said.

"Everything?" he asked, his voice suspiciously nostalgic.

I glanced at the cigar box containing souvenirs of my time with Redford and closed the lid. "All the tax records," I corrected. "I'll bring them to the interview."

"Great. I guess I'd better start making travel plans."

"The interview is a week from Tuesday," I offered.

"Yeah, but I'm interested in buying a stud horse in upstate New York. I was thinking I could come up early and maybe kill two birds with one stone."

So Redford had entered the family business. Another area where we were opposites—the closest I'd ever gotten to a horse was walking next to a carriage in Central Park, and one of the beasts had nipped a hole in my favorite sweater.

"And I've never been to New York City," he continued, "so I thought I'd try to squeeze in some sightseeing since I might never get the chance again. How would you feel about being a tour guide?"

"Fine," I said, then wet my lips. "Are you coming alone?"

"Yes."

My shoulders dropped an inch in relief. I don't know why, but I didn't relish the thought of meeting his new wife. "When would you arrive?"

"Whenever you can fit me in," he said, and God help me, my mind leapt to a time when I had "fit him in" anytime I could.

"How about Friday?" he asked.

"I'll ch-check my schedule, but that should be okay."

"Great," he said, his genial tone making it obvious that our conversation wasn't affecting him at all. "And if you could recommend a place to stay while I'm there, I'd appreciate it."

"I'll look into it," I promised. "How can I reach you?"

He recited a phone number, which I jotted down.

"Although you never know who might pick up around here," he warned with a laugh.

On cue, I heard a shriek of childish laughter and the patter of little feet in the background.

"If you leave a message and you don't hear back from me within a few hours, just call again."

"Sure," I said, my heart dragging. "I'll talk to you soon."

"Okay. Listen, Denise…"

My heartbeat picked up. "Yes?"

"It's great to hear your voice again. I've thought about you a lot over the years and…"

And? I swallowed, waiting.

"And…I'm glad to know you're okay."

I closed my eyes before murmuring, "Same here."

We said goodbye and I disconnected the call on an exhale, feeling wobbly and acknowledging the sudden urge to eat a party-size bag of peanut M&M's. I settled for a cup of nonfat, sugar-free vanilla yogurt with a little cocoa sprinkled over the top (not the same, no matter how much the weight-loss gurus try to convince you otherwise) and tucked myself into a chair with my legs beneath me.

So I was going to see Redford again. I lay my head back on the chair and released a sigh that ended in a moan. Just speaking to him on the phone had left me feeling fuzzy, as if he had brushed his naked body against mine. How pathetic was I that the mere sound of his voice could rattle me after all this time? Especially when Redford had obviously found someone else to brush up against.

I wasn't naïve enough to think that Redford hadn't taken other lovers after our annulment. But because our sexual relationship had been so radical and so… *incomparable* for me, deep down I guess I'd hoped it had been for him, too. That he hadn't played the "kiss you all under" game with anyone else, or that no other woman had left teeth marks in his shoulder.

I laughed at myself. I hadn't really expected Redford to be pining for me, had I?

I mindlessly spooned yogurt into my mouth, sucking on the spoon (which even Freud would have deemed too obvious for analysis), while my thoughts coiled into themselves in confusion. I was scraping the bottom of the container with an eye toward licking the foil lid when the phone rang again.

My pulse jumped—maybe Redford had forgotten to tell me something. I idly wondered if he had kept my phone number and address somewhere, or if he'd simply looked me up through directory assistance. I padded to the bedroom where I'd left the handset and pushed the connect button. "Hello?"

"Hey," Kenzie said. "I called back, but the line was busy."

I wavered, wondering if I should tell anyone about my impending reunion with Redford. But I needed to tell someone, so I spilled my guts.

Kenzie was quiet for a few seconds, then said, "Damn. He's the one with the huge schlong, right?"

I rolled my eyes. "Do we have to go there?"

"Are you prepared to see this man again?"

"Sure," I said, trying to sound casual. "It's no big deal."

"I don't know, Denise. You were really weird when you came back from Las Vegas. Kind of... zombie-like."

A changed woman, like Eve after eating from the Tree of Knowledge. I swallowed hard. "I'll be fine."

"If you say so," she said, but sounded doubtful.

"Subject change. So you were saying that you're not coming back to the city this week."

"Right. I, um, haven't been feeling very well, and I think I'll take it easy here for the next couple of weeks."

"Flu bug?" I asked, flopping onto my bed.

"Actually…it's morning sickness."

A few seconds passed before her words sank in, then I sat straight up. "You're pregnant?"

She laughed. "So it would seem."

"Omigod…congratulations!" Disbelief rolled over me in waves. The fact that one of us was going to be a mother made me feel so…old.

"Thanks, Denise. Sam and I both are thrilled, of course."

"As you should be," I said, feeling myself going misty. "When are you due? Do you know what you're having? Do you have a name picked out?"

Kenzie laughed again. "August, no, and no. Lots of decisions to make between now and then. Oh, there's the other line. Talk to you later in the week?"

"Sure." I congratulated her again on the baby, then hung up, unsettled by Kenzie's declaration, yet knowing it was inevitable that we all move on with our lives. At least, it seemed as if everyone *else* was moving forward. Even Redford had moved on. His phone call proved that *I,* on the other hand, was pathetically mired in the past, more so than I would have thought possible.

With new resolve, I removed the wedding gown from my closet and lifted the plastic. I would need a good photo in order to list the dress on eBay and get top dollar. With trepidation, I undressed, then stepped into the gown and shimmied the satiny dress over my hips. The cool fabric glided over my skin like a caress. I fastened the halter around the nape of my neck, then reached around to pull up the zipper that ended just below my shoulder blades. Minus the leotard, the dress fit even better. I couldn't resist a peek into the full-length mirror sitting in the corner of my cramped bedroom, and at the sight of myself in the ethereal gown, I nearly lost my nerve.

I imagined looking down at the end of the aisle and seeing my groom standing there, his eyes shining with love and desire at the sight of me in this gorgeous gown. Later he would remove the dress with kisses and caresses, his hands and breath so hurried that the gown would have barely fallen to the floor before we were buried inside each other.

I blinked, realizing my arms were covered with goose bumps, and my nipples were budded. I wanted to keep this dress, but doing so would be wasteful and foolish. Just having it in my closet was making me silly and soft. And horny.

So I made myself step away from the mirror and, with relative detachment, set up my digital camera and tripod. I set the timer and posed for three shots in a bridal stance. Then I removed the dress and carefully replaced the plastic with a bittersweet pang. Some woman out there would both appreciate and be able to use the dress, and that gave me a bit of solace.

I pulled up the digital photos, selected the best one and cropped out my head and other extraneous background details. Then I logged on to eBay and listed my impulsive purchase in an eight-day auction, ending next Monday evening. I wanted to be done with the auction before I had to turn my attention to the audit.

> Exquisite designer wedding gown, NWT (new with tags), size ten, creamy white, halter-style dress with pearl-studded skirt and short train, will make any bride feel like a princess on her special day.

I sighed while transferring the details from the tags to the screen. My heart hung low in my chest, but I knew that getting rid of the dress would help to clear my head of past and future marriage fantasies. No wonder Barry wouldn't commit. I was probably giving off "rewind" vibes.

A fact that I repeated to myself over and over as I dressed for our dinner that evening. Since I'd had precious little to eat since the yogurt, my stomach was howling for food. And I had a headache from playing my conversation with Redford over and over in my head. But when I walked up to Barry, who was sitting at the bar in the hushed atmosphere of the posh restaurant, I forced myself to tamp down all thoughts of Redford and the past. Barry was kind, successful, ambitious and…here…in New York…where my life was. One could not underestimate the necessity of proximity to keep a relationship alive.

Barry stood and smiled back, but his eyes reflected something else—regret? Fear? Guilt? He brushed a quick kiss on my mouth and hurriedly threw back the rest of his drink.

Something was wrong…I could sense it. It was obvious from his stiff body language as we followed the hostess to a premium table, as he held out my chair, as he claimed his own seat and snapped the linen napkin over his lap. He didn't seem to want to make eye contact, and he was pulling on his ear—a sure sign that something was on his mind. Tiny alarms sounded in my head as I sipped from my water glass, and my mind started tossing out scenarios to explain his nervous behavior. He'd been offered a job in L.A. Ellen had changed her mind about doing business with Trayser Brothers. Then the truth spanked me:

Barry was going to dump me.

Of course—it made perfect sense. A classy restaurant on a Sunday evening… Break the news in public, then start the week with a clean slate as a single man. Leave town for a few weeks and things would be smoothed over by the time he returned. He'd asked me to meet him to avoid the awkwardness of taking me home afterward, had taken his toiletry bag home to avoid a trip back to my place. I swallowed a mouthful of water with my disappointment, my appetite gone. This was what I got for fantasizing about another man who wasn't even around, while ignoring a perfectly good guy who was right under my nose.

Moving and speaking awkwardly, Barry ordered a pricey bottle of shiraz. I perused the menu, seeing nothing, and watched him under my lashes, my nerves jumping. When the wine arrived and Barry lifted his glass to mine, he made eye contact for the first time.

"To a great friendship," he said, wetting his lips.

Sadness bled through me and I clinked my glass against his, wondering if he would make me wait until the end of the meal to do the deed. But after he drank from his glass, his eyes changed, and I steeled myself for his brush-off.

He reached across the table and clasped my hand. "Denise, we've been together for a while now…long enough, I think."

I nodded, determined to make it easy for him, easy for me.

"Will you marry me, Denise?"

A full ten seconds passed before his words registered. I squinted at him, confused. "Pardon me?"

He grinned. "You're going to make this hard, aren't you?" He swung out of his seat and got down on one knee in front of my chair. A stir sounded around us as other diners turned to stare. He reached into his jacket pocket and removed a black velvet ring box, then opened it to reveal a diamond the size of a peanut M&M. "Denise Cooke, will you marry me?"

My jaw was slack, which I knew wasn't a particularly attractive expression for me, but I couldn't help it. "Stunned" wasn't the right word—I was positively staggered. I felt the eyes of strangers on me, the air heavy with anticipation. Unwittingly, the setting of my first proposal rose in my mind—the bar, the paper clip Redford had bent into a band as a temporary engagement ring until, he'd said, he could retrieve his grandmother's diamond. In retrospect, it all seemed so childish.

I stared at the rock Barry offered me, overwhelmed by his gesture. "It's huge," I murmured.

"It's one of those new laboratory-made diamonds. About one-fourth the cost of a regular diamond."

I tried not to feel deflated. "Oh."

"I knew you'd approve, as frugal as you are."

I nodded. "Of course."

"So," he said, his voice high and tight as he gave a slight nod to the people staring at us. "What do you say, Denise?"

My insides were like hash. I felt like an idiot—I was sure he was trying to break up with me, and the man had been trying to propose! He wanted to *marry* me. It was my second chance to get it right.

I looked into Barry's shining eyes and my heart welled. I knew *this* man's likes and dislikes—that he wanted to have children...someday, and that we would always live in a big city, pursuing our big-city careers. There was no mistake that Barry and I were perfectly suited to one another. I took a deep breath and said, "Yes, Barry...I'll marry you."

6

CINDY AND JACKI stared at my left hand in the middle of the café table, then at me, their lunch salads forgotten.

"Oh, my God," Cindy said. "Barry proposed!"

I nodded. "Last night."

"It's a freaking boulder," Jacki said, her eyes bugged. "He must have spent a fortune."

I decided not to let them in on the "laboratory created" part. They might try to convince me it wasn't romantic to scrimp on an engagement ring. In truth, I appreciated the fact that Barry was saving money for other things, like our wedding, our honeymoon, disability insurance.

Cindy's eyes grew moist. "And this on top of Kenzie's baby news. I'm just so happy."

I squeezed her hand, sending up a little prayer that she'd find a good man soon.

"Have you told Kenzie?" Jacki asked me.

"Not yet," I said, wondering what Kenzie would say, then wondering why I thought she'd be anything but happy for me. "I'm going to call her later."

Jacki raised her water glass. "To the happy couple."

I clinked my glass to theirs in appreciation.

"Well, that's three down, one to go." Jacki winked at Cindy. "You're next."

Cindy smiled wistfully. "I hope so."

"How's the class going?"

"So far, so good. There's a really cute guy in the class who's been talking to me. And I found my *dream* wedding dress Saturday." Then she turned to me, her eyes and mouth rounded. "Oh, Denise—it worked! You buying a wedding gown turned into a self-fulfilling prophecy!"

"Huh?" Jacki said.

I squirmed as Cindy relayed the "running of the brides" stint and how I'd wound up with a gown.

"Did you know Barry was going to propose?" Jacki asked.

I shook my head. "No idea. Evidenced by the fact that yesterday afternoon, I listed the gown on eBay."

Cindy's face fell. "You didn't."

I sighed. "I did. And the reserve price I set has already been met."

Jacki lifted an eyebrow. "Knowing you, the reserve price was more than you paid for it."

"Well, yeah, but it's a great dress. If I'd have known that Barry was going to propose…"

"So cancel the auction," Cindy said.

I frowned. "After bidding starts, I can't." Since I made spending money by selling odds and ends on eBay, I wasn't willing to risk being banned from the online auction house.

"Don't look so glum," Cindy said. "You'll find another dress."

I picked at the fruit on my plate. "It's not just the dress," I said carefully, acknowledging the dread that had kept me awake all night.

"What?" they asked in unison, leaning forward.

"I, um, never quite got around to telling Barry that I was married before."

Jacki's eyebrows shot up. "Really? It never came up?"

I shook my head. "I thought about telling him lots of times, but I was afraid he'd think I was—I don't know—hinting or something."

Jacki pursed her mouth. "Last night might have been a good time to say something."

"He had to leave for L.A. earlier than he expected," I said. "We barely had time to finish dinner." My excuse sounded lame even to my ears. I groaned and dropped my fork onto my plate. "What am I going to do?"

"Call him today and tell him," Jacki said emphatically.

"Yeah, Denise," Cindy said. "Your marriage to Redmon—"

"Redford."

"—only lasted two weeks."

"Six," I corrected.

"Still," she argued. "You had the marriage annulled. That means it never happened."

I smirked. "Only it *did* happen."

Cindy scoffed. "It's not as if you have this secret long-term relationship in your history, or as if your ex-husband is going to show up on your doorstep."

I grimaced. "Well, actually…"

They lunged forward again. "What?"

I told them about the audit letter and the phone call from Redford, my sense of panic increasing as their jaws dropped lower.

"Your ex-husband is coming here?" Jacki asked. "The really hot one with the big Johnson?"

I frowned. "He's not my ex-husband. He's my… non-husband. And I'm afraid if I tell Barry now, he'll think there's unfinished business between me and Redford."

Jacki angled her head. "Is there?"

"No!" I said quickly. "Of course not. Redford has a family."

"He remarried?"

"Yes," I said, then squinted. "Well, he didn't say so exactly, but he mentioned children…girls."

"Marriage and children aren't mutually exclusive," Cindy pointed out.

"Is he still in the Marine Corps?" Jacki asked.

"Retired a few months ago. He joined his family horse business in Kentucky."

"Oh, that's so romantic," Cindy said. "He's a cowboy! Does he wear a hat?"

"I have no idea. He has his life, and I have mine. When this audit is over, we'll never see each other again."

"What about this audit?" Jacki asked. "Are you in trouble?"

"I don't think so. I called the field office this morning to confirm our appointment and from all appearances, it seems pretty routine." At least I hoped so.

"You'd better be careful," Jacki said, pointing her fork at me. "The IRS can ruin your life."

"My cousin Joey had to go to jail for six months," Cindy declared.

I frowned. "That's kind of extreme…did he not even bother to file?"

"Oh, he filed, but a fast-talking tax preparer found all these so-called 'deductions' that saved him a ton of money. Next thing you know, my cousin's being audited and the tax preparer has skipped town. Joey winds up in the clink, with a record for fraud. He lost his job and his wife left him. Sad."

I felt myself go pale. Trayser Brothers would fire me on the spot if I was charged with tax fraud. "I d-don't expect anything like that to happen. But still, I'd like to keep this quiet," I said sheepishly. "My clients might misunderstand."

"Does Barry know?" Jacki asked.

I shook my head.

"So you don't plan to tell Barry about the audit, about Redford, or that you were married?"

"Technically, she *wasn't* married," Cindy argued.

"Not according to the IRS," Jacki murmured, then gave me a probing look before turning back to her salad.

I studied a crouton, feeling guilty and miserable.

"When does the cowboy arrive?" Cindy asked, changing the subject with a sledgehammer.

"Friday."

"The audit is Friday?"

My cheeks warmed. "Um, no, the audit isn't until next Tuesday, but Redford wants to do some sightseeing."

Jacki looked up. "You're taking the man sightseeing?"

My defenses reared. "Just like I've taken dozens of friends sightseeing who've come to the city. And he wants to go look at a stud for sale upstate "

Jacki's mouth jumped at the corners. "And you *always* take visitors stud-shopping."

I frowned. "I'm not going with him, for goodness' sake. I don't even *like* horses."

Jacki nodded, but gave me that look again. "So when does Barry get back in town?"

"He'll be in L.A. for two weeks, maybe three."

"But that's perfect!" Cindy cut in. "Barry never has to know that Redford was even here."

"My thoughts exactly," I said, feeling better. "This whole mistake with Redford will be tied up before Barry gets back."

Jacki nodded thoughtfully. "A good plan," she

conceded, then gave me a sly smile. "As long as you don't repeat your mistake."

I swallowed hard. "No chance of that happening…none at all."

WHEN I GOT HOME from work that evening, I tried to push aside thoughts of calling Redford to firm up his schedule. Procrastinating, I checked my auction on eBay.

When the page loaded, I felt a tiny bit relieved to see that the auction stood at only one bid. True, the bidder had met my reserve price of $275, but maybe I'd attracted a no-pay bidder. Normally, of course, I would report a no-pay bidder, but in this case, I'd be willing to let it slide in order to keep the gown.

Then I zeroed in on the bidder's user ID: SYLVIESMOM. My mouth pinched involuntarily— the woman at Filene's who had tried to pry the gown off my body had said her daughter's name was Sylvie. Could it possibly be the same woman? I looked up the bidder's profile and saw the zip code was within Manhattan…it seemed too much of a co-incidence to be anyone but her.

And call me warped, but I was *not* going to let that woman have my dress, especially when now I could use it myself. I was even more concerned when I saw by the high number next to her user ID that she was a veteran buyer—drat! Then in a moment of blessed revelation, I realized I could simply have a friend,

i.e. Cindy, bid on the gown and win the auction, with
no one the wiser that no money had changed hands.
What I had in mind wasn't ethical if the intent was
to run up the price artificially. But this was an emergency, and I had no intention of taking any money
from Sylvie's mom. I'd only be out the percentage
of the sale I would owe the auction house.

By golly, I was going to win back my dress.

I called Cindy, but before I could tell her what I
had in mind, she blurted, "He called!"

"Who called?"

"The guy from my Positive Thinking class! He
wants to meet for a drink Friday night."

"That's great!" I said and my heart welled for her.
She deserved a terrific guy.

"Maybe buying the wedding dress will work for
me, too," she said, laughing.

I cleared my throat. "Speaking of the wedding
dress, I have a favor to ask."

"What?"

I told her my plan to get my dress back, and she
was hesitant until I told her who the bidder was.

"Ooh! That woman can't possibly have your
dress. What do I have to do?"

I gave her the auction number. "Log on and bid
three hundred dollars. No! Three hundred and *five*
dollars. And thirty-three cents." Bidding in odd
amounts could give a bidder an advantage.

"Okay," she said. "I'll call you back when I'm finished." Because she wasn't an auction/e-mail hound

like me, Cindy had one phone line between her phone and computer.

I watched the auction screen on my computer, hitting the reload button every few seconds until Cindy's user ID, WANTSAMAN, popped up as the high bidder at $280. No matter what amount a bidder enters, eBay will only increment the bid by enough to win the auction. Since the minimum incremental bid at this price point was five dollars, SYLVIESMOM must have bid exactly $275, ergo Cindy's bid automatically adjusting to $280. Aha! With such a tentative initial bid, maybe the woman wasn't that serious about the dress...maybe we would scare her off.

Cindy called back. "Did it work?"

"For now. I'll keep you posted."

"So I forgot to ask you—are your parents excited about your engagement?"

I bit my lip. "I haven't told them yet."

"What? Why not?"

Good question. Even though they were in England, I could have called their cell phone. My mother, Gayle, put X's on the calendar to count down the days of my "fertile years." She liked Barry, and would be beyond ecstatic to learn of our engagement. My dad, Harrison, and Barry had never really clicked. But talking to my dad was like talking to a portly bronze statue. Still, he'd be happy if I were happy.

"They're out of the country. I'll call them...soon."

Cindy sighed. "If I were getting married, my parents would throw a parade."

I laughed. "Maybe this guy from your Positive Thinking class is *the one*."

"Maybe. Meanwhile, let me know if you see a bachelor go on the block on eBay."

"Deal. Talk soon." I said goodbye and hung up, dreading the call to Redford with every fiber of my being. But neither did I want to wait too long and disrupt his family's evening. Chastising myself for the ridiculous butterflies in my stomach, I dialed the number he'd given me and exhaled slowly while it rang.

The phone was picked up, then after much wallowing, a child's voice came on the line. "Heh-wo?"

One of his girls, apparently. "Hello, is your daddy there?"

"Who is dis?"

"Um, this is…a friend…Denise."

"Deece?" the little girl repeated. A man's voice sounded in the background, then more wallowing of the phone ensued.

"Hello?"

My pulse picked up at the sound of his voice— touchably close. "Redford?"

"Denise?"

"Is this a bad time?"

He gave a little laugh. "No. Sorry about that…Janie just learned how to answer the phone."

"No problem." For some reason, I felt weird talking about his children. I cleared my throat. "Did you make flight arrangements?"

"Yes, I'm flying into LaGuardia Friday around noon. Does that work for you?"

From Friday to Tuesday—five days. The last time we'd been together for that amount of time, we'd gotten into a lot of trouble. Of course things had changed drastically...

"Sure, that'll be fine. I called this morning to confirm our appointment at the IRS office Tuesday morning."

"Thanks. What do I need to bring?"

"Maybe your tax forms for the previous year and the following year, just to be safe."

"Will do."

I gave him the name and number of a hotel in my neighborhood. "I thought we could sightsee on Saturday."

"Sounds good."

"I have to work Friday, but I could take my lunch hour to meet you at the airport...if you want."

"That's not necessary," he said. "But I'd like it very much."

My midsection tingled. He'd like very much to see me, or he'd like very much not to navigate the trip into the city alone? "Will I know you?" I asked, and was astounded to hear how breathless I sounded.

"If you ever did," he said, and his words vibrated in the air with sudden intensity.

I swallowed hard. "I'll be wearing—"

"I'll know you," he cut in.

His words struck me as intimate, and my

tongue seemed to adhere to the roof of my mouth. "M-maybe we should exchange cell-phone numbers in case we don't connect outside baggage claim."

"Don't have one," he said cheerfully. "See you Friday."

"Okay," I murmured, then slowly disconnected the call, Redford's voice still reverberating in my head. Why was my skin on fire? My heart crushing against my breastbone? I didn't want to go back to the place I'd been when I was with Redford; to the darker side of myself, when nothing had mattered but being in his arms. My sense of reason had simply fled. It was almost frightening to think back to how bendable I'd been to his wishes, how easily I had trusted him with my future. Was I truly prepared to see Redford again? Would it be cleansing…or climactic?

To assuage my pounding guilt, I picked up the phone and dialed Barry's cell phone, but got his voice mail.

"Hey, it's me," I said. "Just missing you and wanted to hear your voice." I worked my mouth from side to side and considered leaving a blubbery admission about Redford then and there, but decided that was cowardly. Instead I said, "Call me when you can," and pushed the disconnect button.

I stared at my laboratory-engineered diamond ring until my eyes watered. There were so many reasons not to repeat my mistake of falling for Redford. For one, he was unavailable. For two, *I* was unavailable.

We were both unavailable. No mistake about it.

7

Friday
Days left on eBay auction: 4
Bidding on wedding dress up to: $875
Winning bidder: SYLVIESMOM

BY FRIDAY, I still hadn't gotten used to having the engagement ring on my finger. As I waited on the sidewalk outside LaGuardia baggage claim for Redford to emerge, I adjusted the lump beneath my glove to either side, then back to the middle, expending nervous energy. I had barely slept last night, so I was sporting a rather Goth look from the circles beneath my eyes. My stomach held only coffee. And while I stood there telling my silly self to calm down, the biggest mistake of my life strode outside in the cold February sunshine, and the temperature leapt at least two degrees.

My vision blurred, then cleared. Either I was having a stroke, or seeing Redford again was affecting the blood flow to my brain. I remembered him being a handsome guy, but in the three years since I'd seen him, he'd matured into a mountain of a full-grown man, filled out and hardened. Of course, the black Western hat *was* a little imposing, but no less so than the long tan suede duster he wore—a full three cows' worth.

I swallowed hard at the transformation from military officer to horseman. Cindy was right: Redford was a cowboy.

He turned in my direction and his gaze latched on to me. A grin spread over his face revealing white teeth and high dimples. God, I'd forgotten about the dimples...and the impact of his luminous dark eyes. He walked toward me, and I was instantly conscious of my prim ponytail and gray wool coat—a far cry from the mussed hair and denim jacket uniform I'd worn during our brief time together. He'd certainly never seen me in a skirt (although he had seen me in far less). I was surprised he even recognized me... and alarmingly thrilled.

My heart was thudding like crazy when he stopped in front of me, the tails of his open coat swirling around him. Testosterone wafted off him like invisible tethers, tugging at me from all sides. Under the influence of his bronze, virile stare I managed a smile.

"Hello, Redford."

"Hello, Denise," he said, his voice guttural, but smooth. Then he reached up with his be-ringed left hand to remove his hat.

The gesture was so chivalrous, my toes curled. It was just the kind of thing that he had done before to make me feel so feminine and yielding. Beneath the hat, his thick brown hair was a bit longer than the military cut he'd sported when I'd known him. I was startled to see flashes of silver at his temples, a few lines around his amazing eyes. No doubt his experiences in the Gulf had matured him beyond his thirty-eight years. I had offered to meet Redford at the airport because he'd never been to the city. But I suddenly felt foolish because this man had been in places that would make the streets of Manhattan seem like a playground. A pang of gratitude struck me for the sacrifice he'd made, and I felt spoiled for the freedoms I had enjoyed while he'd been overseas. I had the sudden, crazy urge to give myself to him…just like before.

"You look well," I said, my voice unsteady.

"You look beautiful," he said, then leaned forward and dropped a kiss next to my mouth.

The feel of his lips on my skin was startlingly familiar, and I fought the instinct to turn toward his kiss, to meet his lips. I couldn't discern if the contact lasted longer than necessary, or if I was simply processing things in slow-motion. Even after he pulled away, I could feel the weight of his kiss lingering on my skin. When I'd known him before, Redford had elicited a strong visceral response in me, uncommon to *me*, but obviously not uncommon to him, judging from the women around us who literally seemed to lose direction when they saw him.

Everyone in Manhattan was familiar with the Naked Cowboy in Times Square—a scantily-clad guitar-playing tourist novelty—but Redford was the real deal with his khaki shirt tucked into loose, faded jeans, held on to narrow hips with a wide black leather belt. His black roper boots would have received a shine this morning from the horsehair brush his grandfather had given him, I thought as details came flooding back. And the bronze of his skin wasn't the sprayed-on version that many men in New York sported. The fact that I knew what *this* cowboy looked like naked gave me a boost of female satisfaction…and the dangerous stirrings of temptation. Redford clasped my gloved hand and my ring bit into my skin, a not-so-gentle reminder that I had no business being tempted.

"God, it's great to see you, Denise."

I didn't trust my voice…or any other part of my body at the moment, because everything was either tingling, swelling, or vibrating. From the left side of my brain, a rational thought found its way through the mush: *Lack of self-control is precisely how you wound up married to a virtual stranger in the first place.* I conjured up a casual smile that belied my quaking insides. "It's nice to see you, too."

His amazing smile diminished, and I felt a little indignant. Had he expected me to throw myself into his arms and tell him that I'd fantasized about his lovemaking for the better part of three years? The words watered on my tongue before I swallowed them, disgusted with myself. Two minutes into our reunion and I was already unglued.

I averted my glance and was pulled back to the present by the noise of the traffic and jostling pedestrians. It occurred to me that standing outside the airport was a very public place to be seen with a handsome man that my boyfriend had no knowledge of. While the likelihood of someone seeing us was remote, it could happen, considering how much Barry and his colleagues traveled. Panic crushed me for a few seconds while I looked from face to face, expecting any second for someone to recognize me. I cast around for a good reason to get moving. "Hungry?" I asked.

Redford grinned. "Always."

I chose not to read anything into his words. "Okay, let's drop your luggage off at the hotel, then we'll grab a bite to eat."

We joined the line at the taxi stand and I shifted from foot to foot, aware of his eyes on me, trying to think of something to say. The next five days stretched before me like an emotional obstacle course.

"You look different," I said, then gave a nervous little laugh. "I don't know why, but I almost expected to see you in your uniform."

He shrugged. "I just traded one hat for another, I guess. You look different, too."

A warm blush crawled over my cheeks. "You didn't seem to have any trouble recognizing me."

"Oh, you still stand out in a crowd," he said, making me more uncomfortable. "You just seem...more buttoned-up."

His teasing tone needled me. "Just more mature, I suppose," I said.

He made a face. "That's too bad."

I bit my tongue, mostly because I didn't know how to respond. I hadn't expected to be so overwhelmed with resurrected feelings. It was surreal—I knew him, but I didn't know him. We'd been married...then not.

"So you still don't own a car?" he asked, gesturing to the taxi stand.

"More trouble and expense than it's worth," I assured him, knowing how bizarre not owning a vehicle seemed to people who lived in less dense areas. "Besides, I either walk or take public transportation everywhere."

He looked me up and down and a smile lit his black eyes. "So that's how you've managed to stay in such great shape."

My thighs pinged, but I reminded myself that his wife probably wouldn't be thrilled knowing that he was complimenting his ex. Then a disturbing thought hit me—was Redford a ladies' man? Was he thinking that this IRS audit was the chance to reunite with an old flame and stoke the fire a little? I looked at Redford with dismay—had he changed so much? Then another possibility struck me—maybe he hadn't changed at all...maybe I had simply misjudged him when I'd known him.

"Are you okay?" he asked, placing his hat back on his head.

"Fine," I said, resolved that I wouldn't let Redford's powerful sexuality entice me into making another mistake. I stepped up in the taxi line, relieved to see we were next. "Did you make reservations at the hotel I suggested?" I asked, back to a safer topic.

He nodded and stepped off the curb, then walked around to the back of the taxi. Brushing off the cabbie's offer of help, he deposited his leather duffel bag in the trunk himself and closed the lid. "But would you mind if I run a quick errand first?"

Bewildered, I shrugged. "No, of course not."

He handed the cabbie a piece of paper, then held the door open for me to slide in the back seat first. I scooted as close to the opposite door as my bulky coat would allow, but when Redford climbed in, his big body touched mine from knee to shoulder. I decided that pulling away would seem prudish considering our former relationship, so I stared out the window as we drove away and racked my brain for something conversational to say.

"The drive in will at least give you a great view of the city," I offered.

"If I could take my eyes off *you*."

I jerked my head around and, indeed, he appeared to be studying me, his dark eyes earnest beneath the brim of his hat.

The left side of my body was on fire. "What's the errand you need to run?"

"Just a little business transaction," he said easily.

In my purse, my cell phone rang. I pulled it out and glanced at the screen—Barry. My stomach dipped. We'd been playing phone tag for days. I inadvertently glanced at Redford, feeling panicky.

"Don't let me keep you from something important," he said.

The cabbie turned around to verify something on the piece of paper Redford had given him. When Redford leaned forward, I hit the connect button and put the phone to my ear. "Hello?"

"Hi," Barry said. "Did I catch you at a bad time?"

Redford put his hand on my knee, leveraging himself to lean farther forward. I inhaled sharply and my panty hose-clad leg burned beneath his large hand.

"Um, no," I said into the phone. "I was just on my way to…lunch. How are things in L.A.?"

"It's crazy here," he said. "We're working 'round the clock to get a couple of local stations transitioned to our network in time for sweeps. Sorry I haven't been able to call."

"That's okay," I murmured.

"But I spoke to Ellen, and she said you had a good meeting."

I frowned, my first thought being that he'd had time to talk to Ellen, but not to me, then gave myself a mental shake—he had probably talked to her numerous times about work. "I thought it went well," I said. "She took the paperwork with her, so I don't have the account yet, but I think it will happen."

"That's great news."

"Yeah. I owe you big-time."

Barry gave an evocative little laugh. "When I get back, I'll collect."

The juxtaposition of Redford's warm hand on my knee and Barry's voice in my ear sent waves of guilt over me, and I had the crazy urge to blurt a confession right then and there…which, I realized a split-second later, would be disastrous. So I simply took a deep breath and said, "Okay," somewhat woodenly.

"Who are you going to lunch with?" Barry asked over a yawn.

Redford leaned back in the seat and settled next to me with a sexy smile.

I turned my head slightly away from Redford and held the mouthpiece close. "Um…no one you'd know."

"A client?"

Well, I was going to be advising Redford during the tax audit, so indirectly, he *was* a client of mine…sort of. "Yes," I said, peeling my gaze from Redford's long, thick, tanned fingers.

"Then I guess I'd better let you go," Barry said. "Do you have any big plans this weekend?"

"Not really," I squeaked. "I'll be in and out."

I glanced at Redford and he raised his eyebrows suggestively. Heat flooded my face and I was dimly aware of Barry saying something.

"I'm sorry, what was that?"

"I said have fun. I'll talk to you soon."

"Okay." I wondered nervously if being engaged

obligated me to a new, more gushy sign-off. "Bye…you." I winced, my words sounding awkward and ridiculous even to me.

"Bye," Barry said, suppressing another yawn.

I disconnected the call and slid the phone back into my bag, as jumpy as a pussy caught between two toms.

"Bad news?" Redford asked.

I turned toward him, struck anew by the sheer maleness of him. "Hmm? Oh…no."

"You're frowning," he offered. "Is my being here an inconvenience?"

I averted my gaze. "No, of course not."

"You're fibbing," he said. "You probably thought you'd never see me again, and then you get hit with this audit out of the blue. Pretty crazy, huh?"

I looked back and nodded. "It's bizarre."

Then Redford picked up my gloved left hand and looked at me hard. "Have you thought that maybe it could be fate?"

8

I WAS STRUCK SPEECHLESS by Redford's question. Fate? Cindy, with all her romantic ideas about happily ever after, believed in fate. But the concept was too elusive for my linear brain to wrap itself around. Still, for a fleeting second when I looked into Redford's earnest eyes, heaven help me, I wanted to believe that fate had brought us back together. Then I came to my senses and withdrew my hand, emitting a little laugh.

"Redford, somehow I doubt that fate and the IRS are in cahoots. I'd say it's more like mathematical odds." And perhaps my questionable deductions, which I wasn't keen to discuss just yet.

Then he pursed his mouth and nodded. "You're probably right."

When he turned his head to glance out the window, I fought a faint sense of disappointment that he so readily accepted my pragmatic response. Troubled, I studied his profile and was privy to Redford's awestruck expression by the sudden and populous skyline that seemed to stretch into infinity. "It's colossal," he breathed.

My heart swelled with the same pride that I suspect all New Yorkers experience when visitors get their first look at the giant landscape.

"Flying in was dramatic," Redford said, his voice full of wonder. "But seeing it from this perspective, it's almost unbelievable."

I nodded, smiling. "New York is enormous, but everyone finds their little corner and settles in. And after a while you forget how big it is."

He leaned closer to the window to peer up at the towering buildings. A few blocks later, the cab turned down a side street, into a part of the city I'd never traveled. Several turns later, we were definitely off the beaten path, in a retail area that seemed to be dominated by car dealerships and repair shops. The cabbie turned in to a new-car dealership, then turned his head and asked, "This okay?"

"This is fine," Redford assured him, opening the door.

I frowned, confused. "Shall I hold the cab and wait for you?"

Redford shook his head and extended his hand. "That won't be necessary. We're driving out of here."

I put my hand in his, and even the nubby yarn of my glove wasn't enough to dull the zing of touching him. "You're buying a car?"

"A truck," he corrected, then closed the door. Again he waved off the cabbie's help with his bag and paid the bill, adding a tip large enough to disturb me. Redford shook the cabbie's hand, then gave a friendly wave as the car pulled away. The driver waved back, clearly puzzled. I squelched a smile, thinking the cabbie would no doubt tell his wife that evening about the Southerner who handled his own bag, overtipped, shook his hand and waved goodbye.

"Redford," I murmured. "You tipped that man a hundred percent."

Redford shrugged good-naturedly. "It's only money."

I stood flat-footed as shock waves rolled over me. *It's only money?* Redford personified my nightmare client. I had, of course, noticed his tendency to be loose with money during the time we'd been in Vegas, but I'd rationalized that it was *Vegas*. Even I had gotten caught up in the partying, freewheeling atmosphere. I'd lost thirty-five dollars on slots the first day...oh, and I'd wound up married. But in hindsight, Redford had been happy to let me take care of our taxes—was he a financial train wreck?

While I pondered that disconcerting line of thought, Redford smiled and shouldered his leather duffel bag, then headed toward the sales office. I trailed behind, more than a little uncomfortable. I'd never purchased a car before, but I'd heard enough horror stories from friends to know that it would be easy to be taken for a ride, so to speak.

And, sure enough, the salesman had seen Redford coming. He came over and the men shook hands as if they knew each other. By the time I caught up to them, the salesman was moving toward an area where gigantic pickup trucks were parked. Redford introduced me to "Jim," who was handsome in a slick kind of way, and I nodded politely.

"Ah, so this is the little woman," Jim said in a sales-y voice.

I opened my mouth to object, but Redford suddenly squeezed me close with a one-armed hug and laughed. "That's right." After a few seconds of utter confusion, I realized that Redford was working the salesman by pretending we were married in preparation for the good cop/bad cop negotiating blitz. I brightened—I could negotiate a bargain. I lived for chances to be bad cop.

"I believe this is what you asked for," Jim said, patting the hood of a gigantic red pickup with an extra-large cab that looked as if it could tow a house.

While Redford walked around the truck, nodding his approval, I sneaked a glance at the sticker price and nearly swallowed my tongue. Not only could the truck *tow* a house, it cost almost as much as one. I opened my mouth to start my bad cop monologue and Redford said, "I'll take it."

"Great," Jim said, beaming.

Since my mouth was already open, I gaped in horror. Sticker price? He was going to pay sticker price?

"Um, *honey,*" I said demurely, squeezing Redford's arm and, God help me, not hating it, "maybe we should discuss this."

Redford's eyebrows raised slightly and he seemed amused. "Discuss what, *sweetie?*"

I shot daggers at him behind the salesman's back. "The price," I said between clenched teeth.

But he only laughed and patted my hand. "Like I said, it's only money."

I felt faint, both from the teasing interplay and his irreverence. The financial demon in me reared her frugal head. "But, *honey,* remember we might have an unexpected expense coming up next week."

"*Sweetie,* you worry too much," he chided, his dark eyes half-serious. "I'll take care of everything."

His voice was so level, so calming that I actually believed him. I was breaking one of the cardinal rules I gave to my female clients: Don't assume your boyfriend/husband/significant other knows more about money than you do. With a jolt I remembered just how susceptible I was to Redford's charm. It was his money, after all—he had the right to spend it anyway he pleased.

Yet I didn't want Redford to be in arrears with the IRS. If my creative accounting was the root cause of any fines, I would offer to pay for everything, of course...although if it were more than a nominal amount, I wouldn't be able to...unless Ellen Brant opened an account at Trayser Brothers.

Thinking of Ellen made me think of Barry and all that I was keeping from him. Guilt washed over me anew—I was engaged to Barry, yet hadn't hesitated to pretend to be Redford's wife for the sake of saving a few bucks.

And the ease with which Redford and I had fallen into calling each other pet names was even more unsettling. Redford had often called me "sweetie" when we were together. Adrenaline rushed through my veins—I felt like I had stepped into quicksand, and was already up to my manhandled knees.

"Right this way," Jim said, his voice triumphant with a new sale. Then he turned to me and said, "Denise, you're exactly how Redford described you."

I blinked. "Pardon me?"

"Jim and I served together in Iraq," Redford said, his expression somewhat sheepish.

"He talked about you nonstop," Jim said, grinning.

I was shot through with shock and some other sensation that was unidentifiable—pleasure? Satisfaction? Dismay?

"Jim," Redford cut in, clapping the man on the back, "you wouldn't want me to start telling stories on *you* now, would you?"

Jim laughed outright. "No. I guess we all pulled a few stupid stunts while we were away from home, didn't we?" They shared a belly laugh as they walked to the sales office.

I stayed in the showroom to allow Redford to sign the paperwork and to allow myself time to absorb what Jim had said. Redford had talked about me to his buddies? Nonstop? Why had that declaration shaken me so? Because I had assumed that Redford had returned to his unit and lamented the big mistake he'd made by marrying a virtual stranger in Vegas, that's why. Of course, maybe he had chalked it up to one of the "stupid stunts" that Jim had mentioned.

Confused, I dropped into a chair, and pulled out my cell phone. I considered called Kenzie, but she had reacted strangely when I'd told her that Barry had proposed, and even more so when I'd told her about Redford's visit. In truth, we'd had quite a spat about mistakes I'd made and mistakes she was afraid I would make again. Until her hormones leveled out, I was prepared to keep my distance. Instead, I dialed Cindy.

She answered on the first ring. "Hello?" Her voice lilted with hope, and I hated to disappoint her that it was just me calling and not the guy from her Positive Thinking class.

"Hey, it's Denise."

"Hi! I'm having lunch with Jacki, and the suspense is killing us! Have you seen Redford? Does he look the same?"

I touched my hand to my temple. "Yes, I've seen him, and he looks…the same."

Cindy covered the mouthpiece and I could hear her say, "She's seen him and he looks the same!" then came back. "Wait—Jacki wants to listen, too. Okay, go ahead. You were saying he looks the same?"

"Maybe a tad better," I admitted, thinking of the black hat.

"Does he still have the Washington Monument in his pants?" Jacki asked dryly.

"I'm hanging up."

"No, wait!" Cindy shouted. "Jacki was kidding. What was it like when you saw each other again? Did you see fireworks?"

Jacki scoffed. "Enough with the fantasy, Cindy."

"Wait a minute," Cindy said in a huff. "Jacki, aren't you the woman who found Mr. Right based on the pair of *shoes* he was wearing? You have a *season pass* to fantasyland."

I rolled my eyes at their banter. "Hello? Can you two argue on your own airtime?"

"Denise, did you see each other across a crowded room?" Cindy persisted. "Did the world stop?"

"Oh, brother," Jacki muttered.

But I had to admit that those strange tingling sensations mounted in my chest again. "It was a little awkward, I suppose." I sighed. "I...I don't know why I called."

"Are you in love with him again?" Cindy asked dreamily.

"Of course she isn't," Jacki retorted, then added, "Are you, Denise?"

"Of course I'm not," I assured her. "I guess I'm just feeling a little out of sorts."

"That's because he was your first love," Cindy declared.

Jacki scoffed. "Does your first love happen to be wearing a ring?"

"Yes."

"What a coincidence, both of you wearing rings."

"I got it, Jacki," I said wryly. "Don't worry, nothing is going to happen."

"Where is he now?" Cindy asked.

"Buying a new pickup truck."

They gasped. "Just like that? He got off the plane and is buying a new truck?"

"And he paid sticker price," I added miserably.

They gasped again.

"Denise, I know that full retail is painful for you to watch," Jacki said gently, "but it's more proof that the marriage would've never worked." She sighed. "I know you've never quite gotten over Redford, but this audit is the best thing that could have happened. The more time you spend with Redford, the more you'll realize that getting an annulment was the right thing to do. Besides, he's married…and you have Barry now."

My shoulders fell in relief. "You're right. Of course, you're right. I knew you two would make me feel better."

"How's the bidding on the dress?" Cindy asked.

I frowned. "When I checked this morning, SYLVIESMOM was winning. Will you log on and bid again when you have time?"

"Absolutely," Cindy said. "You *will* wear that dress when you walk down the aisle!"

I smiled into the phone. "Thanks, girls. I'll call you soon. Cindy, have fun tonight on your date."

I disconnected the call and spent the next few

minutes practicing deep breathing and relaxation techniques.

I will not make the same mistake twice. I will not make the same mistake twice.

A few minutes later, I was feeling slightly more in control. But when the office door opened and Redford came out grinning and, from one evocative finger, dangling the keys to his new ride, my Zen fled.

"Ready to go?" he asked.

I nodded, trying to banish wicked, wicked thoughts from my mind. I followed him toward the monster truck, trotting to keep up with his long stride. He opened the passenger-side door for me and before I knew what was happening, he'd put his hands on my waist to lift me onto the tan leather seat. I gasped and instinctively put my hands on his shoulders. Our bodies connected like a plug and socket—instant voltage. My gaze locked with his; my breath frozen in my chest.

Redford seemed to be having trouble breathing as well, attested by the long, uneven white puffs in the frigid air of the cab. His hands tightened around my waist as he settled me into the seat. The leather must have been cold, but I couldn't feel anything except the warmth radiating from his body. My knees hit him chest level, my coat and skirt rucked up past my knees several inches to expose my thighs. I had a vision of another time when Redford had set me on a table for the purpose of devouring me. From the slightly hooded look in his eyes, I wondered if he were remembering, too.

I gulped air and gave a little cough, releasing his shoulders and squirming against his hands. He let go of my waist and stepped back, but gave my legs a lingering glance before closing the door. I exhaled noisily and counted to five. Considering our history, it was natural for us to experience a little awkward attraction…wasn't it? But we were adults…we could deal with it.

By the time I'd righted my clothing, he had tossed his duffel bag into the back seat of the cab and climbed into the driver's seat, where he began making adjustments to accommodate his long legs. If our brush with flirtation had affected him, he had dismissed it easily enough.

"I hope you don't mind navigating," he said, placing his hat on the seat between us. "It might take me a few hours to get my bearings."

"I don't mind," I said, still shaken.

"So, what do you think about my truck?"

"It's…red."

"Red is the color of DeMoss Stables."

I nodded. "Ah. And it's…big. I've never seen a pickup with a back seat."

"It's called a quad-cab."

"Oh."

His brows knitted. "You don't like it?"

I laughed and gestured vaguely at the dashboard that looked big enough to belong to an aircraft. "Redford, it's your truck. But you barely glanced at it before you bought it. Do you always make such rash decisions?"

His jaw tensed and, too late, I realized that in light of our past, my question seemed at once unnecessary *and* judgmental.

"Apparently so," he said quietly, then turned the key in the ignition, bringing the engine to life. He turned his dark eyes in my direction. "But then I usually know what I want when I see it."

The moisture evaporated from my mouth. I couldn't seem to drag my gaze from his. I was mired in confusion, tongue-tied. Was he referring to me? To our marriage? Did I want to know?

"Better buckle up," he said breezily.

Glad to have something to keep my hands occupied, I tugged on the buckle. But the strap was stuck from never being used.

"Here, let me," he said, and leaned across the seat, brushing past me to grab the strap, trapping me between the seat and his big body. His face was mere inches from mine, the scent of strong, musky soap tickling my nose. I squirmed, which, to my dismay, resulted in rubbing my chest against his. My cheeks burned as if we were naked, instead of wearing heavy coats. Just having him in proximity was wreaking havoc with my self-control.

A lazy smile lifted Redford's mouth as he pulled the belt over my shoulder and clicked it home next to my thigh. "I wouldn't want anything bad to happen to you on my watch."

I gave him a watery smile of thanks and prayed that he couldn't tell how much he was getting to me.

I wasn't in the business of feeding the ego of married men. A glance at the gold band on his left hand was enough to boost my resolve.

He turned on the heater, fastened his own seat belt, then goosed the engine a couple of times before pulling out of the lot. "Which way?"

I looked around to get oriented, then pointed right. I waited until he had pulled into traffic before asking, "Redford, what was that all about back there?"

"What do you mean?"

I wet my lips. "Allowing that guy to think we were…married."

He studied the road, then made a rueful noise. "Jim and I knew each other when I returned from my leave in Las Vegas three years ago." He shrugged. "Maybe it was wrong, but since you were with me, it just seemed easier to pretend than to explain that you and I were no longer…together." He looked over at me. "I'm sorry if it embarrassed you."

Considering I hadn't told Barry or my parents the complete truth either, I wasn't exactly in a position to judge. "No, it's…okay." Antsy, I glanced at my watch.

"Am I making you late?" he asked.

"No. I told my boss I'd be taking an extended lunch," (actually, I had told him I was on the trail of a big account), "but I'll need to get back soon."

"Do you still have time to eat?"

I wasn't the slightest bit hungry, but with some alarm I realized I wasn't yet ready to leave Redford's company. We had so much to discuss, yet so many things I didn't want to talk about. The audit. His family. My engagement. I guess deep down I knew that talking about those things would put an end to the flirtation that I was enjoying on some very base level.

Plus, I realized in astonishment, it would also put an end to the impossible fantasy I had been harboring in the recesses of my mind: that someday Redford would come for me.

The thought hit me so hard, I blinked back sudden moisture. I had discovered something about myself that I didn't want to know. What part of myself had I been withholding from friends and potential lovers since I had returned from Vegas three years ago? What part of myself had I given to Redford…and would I ever get it back?

"Earth to Denise."

I looked over at him. "What?"

His smile was gentle. "I asked if you still have time to eat."

My throat constricted. "Yes, I have time to eat."

The sooner we got things out on the table, the better.

The times we had made love on a table notwithstanding, of course.

"Good," he said. "Afterward I'll drop you off at your office."

"No," I said quickly, then gave a little laugh. "That's not necessary—my office is close to the restaurant I had in mind." A lie, but I couldn't risk anyone seeing me being dropped off by a good-looking stranger driving a red monster truck. I wouldn't want word getting back to Barry. My fiancé. The guy who was available and loved my mind. The guy with whom I had so much in common.

Redford winked and slanted a sexy smile in my direction. "Whatever the lady wants."

I feigned fascination with a passing landmark to cover my traitorous internal reaction. Blast that devilish smile of his! As the interior of the truck warmed I exhaled slowly, settling into the leather seat, forcing myself to relax one muscle at a time. I wasn't going to think about the days stretching before us— I was going to deal with Redford one hour at a time.

But it's over a hundred hours until he leaves, my mind whispered.

I was in big trouble.

9

"TABLE FOR TWO?" the hostess of Rutabaga's asked me, although she could barely take her eyes off Redford.

"Yes," I said, slightly irked. The man was like a tranquilizer dart.

She checked a seating chart and smiled past my shoulder at Redford. "It'll be just a few moments."

I smirked and stepped back into the knot of people who were also waiting for a table. Redford had removed his hat and was studying the dark, oaky decor, although not as closely as he was being studied by every female in the place...me included.

To say that Redford stood out was an understatement—with his stark good looks, brawny build and Western-flavored clothing, he looked as if he'd just walked off a movie set. My mind flashed to the movie *Crocodile Dundee,* where a bushman visits Manhattan for the first time. Like the character in the movie, Redford seemed oblivious to the attention he attracted.

"Looks like a nice place," he offered. "Do you eat here often?"

"Sometimes," I lied.

Actually, I'd chosen the eatery for its proximity to Redford's hotel, its carnivorous menu, its tucked away location and its high, dark booths...not that I expected to see anyone I knew. For as long as I'd lived in New York, I could count the times I had actually run in to someone I knew—unless it was a regular haunt—on one hand.

"Denise! Fancy meeting you here!"

I froze, then turned to see Sam Long, Kenzie's veterinarian husband, walking toward me holding a carryout bag. Sam taught at a clinic in the city three days a week to be close to Kenzie, who was holed up in Jar Hollow this week with morning sickness.

I managed a smile. "Hi, Sam."

He gave me a quick hug. "Hey, congratulations on your engagement—Kenzie's been talking about it all week."

I felt Redford's gaze snap to me and I sensed him inch closer. For reasons I couldn't fathom, I found myself wishing that Sam hadn't said anything, although the subject was bound to come up sooner or later. And considering the inappropriate feelings that Redford had resurrected in me, sooner was better.

"Thanks, Sam," I murmured. "Congratulations to you on the baby."

A grin split his face. "Amazing, huh? I'm still trying to get used to the idea of being a father. I guess this is a big week for all of us." He looked around. "Is Barry with you?"

"Er, no," I squeaked.

"Traveling again? Well, he doesn't deserve you," Sam said cheerfully. "But then I married up, too."

Sam and Barry had never really hit it off, which had concerned me a little simply because I was so close to Kenzie and wanted us all to get along. But Kenzie had assured me that Sam was shy and didn't normally warm up to people right away.

Redford cleared his throat, and Sam looked back and forth between us, clearly puzzled.

I inhaled deeply. "Sam Long, meet Redford De-Moss. Sam is married to one of my best friends, Kenzie, and Redford is...an old friend."

Realization dawned on Sam's face. "Oh, right, Kenzie said something about your ex coming to town, some kind of tax business, right? Nice to meet you," he said to Redford.

Redford extended his hand. "Same here."

"You're from Kentucky?"

"That's right."

"Know anything about horses?"

Redford smiled and his stance eased. "A fair bit. You?"

I watched in amazement as the two men fell into conversation like old buddies, throwing around horse terminology, each visibly excited to find a kindred spirit. Sam had specialized in equine research and lived on a farm in upstate New York where he ran a small-town veterinary practice.

"I'm heading up to Valla Farms Sunday to check out a teaser stud," Redford said.

"That's only about thirty miles from my place," Sam said. "I'd be happy to go along and look him over for you."

"I'd be much obliged," Redford said.

"Denise, are you riding up, too?" Sam asked. "I know Kenzie would be thrilled to see you."

I shook my head. "I wasn't planning to—"

"Come with me," Redford said, his voice husky... challenging.

I swung my gaze up to meet his and saw something had clouded his eyes—disappointment? Determination? I was thoroughly confused. And intrigued.

"Unless you have other plans," he added mildly.

Sam gave a little laugh. "I would consider it a personal favor, Denise. Kenzie could use some company."

Redford lifted one eyebrow in question, and I wavered. In the nearly one year since Kenzie had commuted to Jar Hollow on the weekends, I had never visited her home there. My excuse had always been that I didn't have a car. But since Redford was going to be stopping there, it seemed ridiculous for me not to go. Besides, it might help to smooth things over with Kenzie.

I gave a cautious little shrug. "Okay."

"Great," Sam said. "I'll let Kenzie know." He gave Redford directions, then extended his hand again. "Nice to meet you, man. I think it's great that the two of you can put the past behind you and still be friends."

Redford shook Sam's hand and nodded. "See you Sunday."

"Your table is ready," the nearly giddy hostess announced to Redford.

With my tongue in my cheek, I followed her to a booth. Redford walked just behind me, his hand hovering at my waist. He helped me out of my coat, casting a lingering glance at my engagement ring when I removed my gloves to stuff them in the pockets. Then he removed his own coat and hat and hung them on a nearby rack. I watched him, guiltily stealing a glance at the way his jeans hugged his lean hips from behind, the way the muscles in his back played beneath his shirt. The man could turn the most simple movements into sexy athleticism.

I realized my mouth was watering, and not from the aroma of steak in the air. I pinched my thigh to derail my wayward thoughts and had conjured up a casual smile by the time he returned to slide into the booth, sitting opposite me. A waitress showed up to take our drinks order, then left us alone in an awkward, tense silence.

"Your friend's husband seems like a nice guy," Redford offered.

"He is," I agreed.

"And you're engaged to be married."

I blinked, then lifted my chin. "As a matter of fact, I am."

He reached over and picked up my left hand to study the engagement ring Barry had given me. The callused tips of his fingers brushed my sensitive palm, sending waves of awareness shooting up my arm. It was all I could do not to pull my hand back.

He rubbed his thumb over the large stone. "Wow. Impressive."

With some effort, I found my voice. "Thank you."

"It looks flawless. And it's much bigger than the one I would have given you," he said, nodding.

His grandmother's ring. He had promised to get it from his family safe and bring it with him on his next leave. I flushed, feeling shallow, and pulled my tingling hand from his. Self-consciously, I put my left hand in my lap and fingered the hem of my napkin.

He picked up the menu. "So, how long have you been engaged?" His voice was tinged with…anger? Impossible.

I picked up my menu. "Not long."

"Did I hear Sam say a week?"

I frowned. "Why the inquisition, Redford?"

He shrugged, still perusing the menu. "Because when I asked you on the phone if you'd gotten remarried, you said you hadn't."

I raised my eyebrows. "I haven't."

"And that you live alone."

"I do. Redford, if I didn't know better, I'd say you were…irritated that I've moved on with my life."

He glanced up at me, his mouth set in a straight line.

"B-but that would be ridiculous," I stammered. "B-because you're married with a family."

"Excuse me?" He dropped his menu.

"Well, aren't you?"

"No! What on earth gave you that idea?"

I dropped my menu. "Because you said…on the

phone…that you were in Versailles…because your girls were there."

His face crumpled in laughter. "I meant my nieces." His eyes twinkled. "And my mares."

My pulse raced wildly. I was at a loss for words, until my gaze rested on his left hand. I pointed at the irrefutable evidence. "What about your wedding ring?"

He looked down. "Oh. That."

"Yeah…*that.*"

He slid it off his finger and pushed it across the table toward me. "It's the one you gave me, Denise."

I stared at the plain gold band as if it were booby-trapped. My mind reeled. "You kept your ring?" *Didn't you?* my conscience whispered.

"I put it in storage and just never got around to doing anything with it. I thought you might want it back to, you know, melt down into a nugget or something."

"A nugget?"

"Isn't that the fashionable thing to do with wedding rings once the marriage is over? Make a nugget pendant out of the ring?"

I shook my head. "I have no idea."

"Some of my Marine buddies who were married more than once just kept adding to theirs." He laughed. "One guy's nugget got so big, he had a belt buckle made out of it."

I pursed my mouth. "Impressive." And it reinforced the information reported in the newspaper article that had prompted me to file for the annulment—soldiers liked to get married.

He sobered and cleared his throat. "You can take it. Sell it if you like."

Glinting under the light of the pendant fixture that hung over the table, the plain band of gold looked new. The large circumference of the ring reminded me of how difficult it had been to find a band to fit Redford's thick finger…the man had large hands. Hands that knew how to do indescribable things to me. With great effort, I brought my mind back to the present.

"You sent *my* ring back with the annulment papers," I murmured.

"I figured you could sell it to help pay the legal fees."

I pressed my lips together and nodded, unable to admit that I had kept the ring…and not just because I'd forgotten about it.

He picked up his ring and extended it toward me. "Do you want it?"

I swallowed and shook my head.

He nodded matter-of-factly, then tucked the ring into his shirt pocket, where it pushed against the polished cotton. The rounded neck of a snowy white T-shirt peeked just above the top button of his khaki-colored shirt…under his jeans he would be wearing equally white boxer shorts. The elastic waistband would ride just below a tiny mole on his left hip. My mind seemed determined to delay processing Redford's bombshell of a revelation.

"So," I said slowly, "you're…not…married?"

He held my gaze. "Nope. But you're engaged."

"Right."

His dark eyes were unreadable, his expression still. My emotions ran the gamut from nervous to miffed to flattered to worried. I'd agreed to spend time with Redford because I'd thought he was married and it seemed...safe. Now, I wasn't so sure.

The waitress came to leave our drinks—water for me, sweet iced tea for Redford—and to take our orders. My stomach was in such turmoil, I couldn't conceive of eating, but I ordered soup to appear normal. Conversely, Redford ordered a porterhouse steak, baked potato, mixed vegetables and a chef's salad with extra cheese.

When the waitress left, he rested his elbows on the table. "So...who's the lucky guy?"

I took a drink of water from my glass. "His name is Barry Copeland. He's a television producer."

He nodded. "Sounds exciting. How long have you known him?"

"A couple of years."

He gave a little smile. "I guess that's the proper amount of time to know someone before you get married."

I nodded. "I...suppose so."

"Have you set a date for the wedding?"

"No."

"Are you going to do it up right this time with a fancy dress and lots of attendants?"

I squirmed, thinking about that darned dress hanging in my closet. "We haven't discussed it, really."

"I heard you tell Sam that your boyfriend was out of town."

"That's right. He's in L.A. for a few days."

He pressed his lips together. "He doesn't know that I'm here, does he?"

I shifted in my seat and tried to look indignant. "What makes you think that?"

"Because no man in his right mind would leave town while his fiancée plays hostess to her ex-husband."

"Redford, you're not my ex-husband," I said lightly.

"Oh, right—the annulment." He leaned back in the booth and pulled on his chin. "A signed piece of paper that says nothing happened between us doesn't make it so. I was there, Denise…something happened."

Beneath the table, I had frayed the end of the napkin with my frantic picking. "That was a long time ago, Redford. I was…different."

His dark eyebrows lifted. "Different? Different how?"

A flush climbed my throat and heated my face inch by inch. I realized that I needed to be blunt for my own salvation. I leaned forward for the sake of discretion and chose my words carefully. "People sometimes do strange things when they're in a place where they don't know anyone. I'm not the woman that you knew in Las Vegas…that was…temporary."

His eyes narrowed slightly. "Temporary?"

I nodded. "A…phase."

He pursed his mouth and leaned forward until our faces were mere inches apart. "You're telling me," he said, his voice low and husky, "that the amazingly sexy, sensual woman I knew and married in Las Vegas no longer exists?"

His words stroked my skin like the blade of a knife—raising gooseflesh and promising peril if I made a wrong move. His eyes were dark and teasing…tempting. Challenging me to be that woman again—the one who'd given him full power over her body and done things she'd only read about, the one who'd fallen under his spell so completely that she'd thrown caution to the wind and married a man with whom she had nothing in common. Only one answer made sense, but I wavered, lured by the promise in his eyes that we could pick up where we'd left off. Five days of pure carnal bliss.

I opened my mouth and the words stalled on my tongue. I moistened my dry lips. "Redford…"

The tip of his tongue appeared to wet his lips. "Yes?"

"Here's your food," the waitress announced.

I sat back and watched awkwardly while she deposited various plates and bowls in front of us. I felt light-headed from the pressure of the decision at hand.

When she left, Redford was still staring at me. "You were saying, Denise?"

I inhaled deeply, then exhaled. "I was saying that you're right, Redford. That woman doesn't exist."

The light went out of his eyes, but he smiled none-theless. "Okay. You don't have to worry—I'll be-have myself." He picked up his fork and knife. "Are we still on for sightseeing tomorrow?"

I nodded slowly, relieved that Redford had ac-cepted my explanation without question. Maybe we could be friends after all…. And we still had to get through the audit on Tuesday. "You'll be okay by yourself tonight?"

His eyebrows shot up, then an amused smile curved his mouth. "I'll manage."

My cheeks flamed. "I didn't mean—"

"Relax, Denise. I didn't expect you to entertain me every minute that I'm here. Jim's coming by tonight and we're going to get a drink, maybe find a cigar bar."

Go out on the town, find a couple of girls? To which he had every right, I told myself. "You still smoke?"

He nodded, then grinned. "I'm afraid you'll find me pretty much the way I was when you knew me before."

My thighs tingled. He was mocking my assertion that I was different now. I carefully picked up my soup spoon. "So I'll come by your hotel in the morn-ing, say around ten?"

"I'll be ready," he said, all pleasant politeness.

I watched as he dove into his food with the enthu-siasm I remembered—the enthusiasm with which he approached everything in life, including sex. Once upon a time, he had tackled my body with animalistic energy. It had changed my life…for a few precious days. He'd just let me know that he was willing to take me to that place again, where nothing mattered except how good we made each other feel.

I focused on spooning some type of soup into my mouth, but my hand was shaking. I just hoped that Redford wouldn't notice.

10

WORK FRIDAY afternoon was a blur. I spent most of
it staring at my computer screen, (I received a quick
e-mail from Barry who said he'd call later), and com-
municating with Ellen Brant's voice mail (saying I
was looking forward to hearing from her and final-
izing the paperwork for her investment account). Ellen's assistant finally called me back and asked if we
could meet Tuesday afternoon. I couldn't imagine the
audit taking all day, so I agreed. I should have felt
happy, but honestly, I felt lousy that I was taking advantage of an opportunity that Barry had arranged,
yet I was keeping so much from him. I typed a chatty,
understanding e-mail reply to Barry, then looked up
laboratory diamonds on the Internet, telling myself
I needed to be familiar with the emerging industry if
an investment opportunity presented itself.

The technology was fascinating—a machine com-
pressed carbon under extreme pressure to form a diamond, in two days replicating the same process that
took nature thousands of years to achieve, except the
"laboratory" diamond was flawless. (So Redford had

been right.) Diamond mine owners were concerned about the competition, but seemed sure that most customers would prefer "real" diamonds, citing that eternal love was best represented by a naturally formed stone. Creators of the engineered diamonds, however, argued that love was best represented by a flawless stone.

I bit my lip, frowned and logged off.

On the walk home, I found myself looking at my surroundings as Redford might: leaning my head back to gaze at the buildings, taking time to notice the street vendors, even splurging on a bouquet of Gerber daisies, which were scandalously expensive this time of year. I resisted, however, buying a bag of peanut M&M's. If I had the willpower to turn down Redford's offer of a sexual escapade, I could resist anything.

When I arrived home, the tickets to Las Vegas that I'd ordered for me and Barry were in the mail—a reminder that I had made the right decision concerning Redford. I found a vase for the flowers and nuked a wedge of low-fat lasagna—my scant lunch had left me starving. While I ate, I booted up my laptop to check my wedding-dress auction, then frantically dialed Cindy.

"SYLVIESMOM is winning!" I said. "You have to bid higher!"

"How high do you want me to go?"

"It doesn't matter, because there won't be a transaction. Just keep bidding!"

"Okay."

I looked at my watch. "Wait a minute—aren't you supposed to be having a drink with the guy from your class?"

She sighed. "He called and asked for a rain check. He said something had come up. Personally, I think he got a better offer."

"That's not possible," I murmured, furious with the jerk. "Want to come over?"

"Thanks, but I told my neighbor I'd help her paint her bathroom. You're not entertaining Redford tonight?"

"No," I said, too quickly.

She picked up on it. "Did something happen after we talked?"

"No," I said, then swallowed. "Well…yes. I found out that Redford's not married."

"Really?"

"No wife, no kids."

"*Omigod*—maybe he's still in love with you!"

I emitted a strangled laugh. "Cindy, that's ridiculous. If he were in love with me, don't you think he would've gotten in touch with me before now?"

"Maybe he was afraid you'd reject him."

I laughed again. "Trust me—Redford is afraid of nothing."

"So, if he's not in love with you, what does it matter if he's available?" Then she gasped. "You're not still in love with him, are you?"

"No!" I snapped. "I…well, it just makes me uncomfortable, spending so much time with him now that I know."

"Are you afraid of him?"

"God, no. Redford would never hurt me."

"Then what? You don't trust him?"

"No, of course I trust him. Redford is the most honorable man I know."

"Ah…you don't trust yourself."

"No— I…" I stopped and took a deep breath. "I feel guilty gallivanting around with a single man behind Barry's back."

"Denise, going to the Empire State Building isn't gallivanting. Besides, it's just one day."

"Two days—I'm going stud-shopping with Redford on Sunday."

"Come again?"

"We ran into Sam today, and the horse farm is close to his place, so I'm riding up with Redford to see Kenzie."

"Sounds logical to me."

I chewed on my lip, then exhaled. "You're right. It's completely logical. I'm making too big a deal out of this, aren't I?"

"Yes."

"Thank you. Have fun painting. Oh, and don't forget to raise your bid!"

"I will!"

I hung up, digesting Cindy's sensible words, then alternated between compulsively checking my dress auction and picking up the phone to call Barry and rat on myself. Instead, I dialed my mother's cell phone, expecting to leave a message, astounded when she actually answered.

"Hello?"

"Hi, Mom. It's Denise."

"Denise, what a nice surprise. Is anyone dead, dear?"

I frowned. "Uh…no."

"Oh, I thought you might be calling with bad news. I had a premonition this morning that I was going to hear bad news today. Didn't I, Harrison?"

I could picture my dad nodding. This wasn't going well. "Actually, Mom, I called to tell you that…Barry and I are engaged."

My mother shrieked and covered the mouthpiece. "Harrison—our daughter is getting married!" She came back on the line. "Oh, Denise, we're so happy for you! Aren't we happy for her, Harrison?"

"We're happy for you, sweetheart," my father shouted in the background.

"Have you set a date?" my mother asked.

"No—"

"Oh, you'll have to get a dress! Oh, won't that be fun!"

Thinking of the gown hanging in my closet, I massaged my temple. "Yes. How's your trip?"

"Horrible," my mother declared, then launched into a diatribe about how miserable the weather had been. "*Noah* never saw such rain. I've been wet through and through since the minute we arrived."

I had made appropriate sympathetic noises, then told her to call me when they returned to the States and gave them my love. She was shouting, "My daughter's getting married!" to her friends before she even disconnected the call.

I felt like crap.

What would my mother think of me if she knew that I'd already been married once?

Not *married,* I chided—my marriage to Redford had been *annulled.* Obliterated. Expunged. It didn't exist.

Which wouldn't be so hard to believe if Redford DeMoss wasn't so very, very real. And so very, very sexy. I closed my eyes and remembered the way he had leaned across the table, baiting me with those amazing eyes to let down my guard, to let him in— literally—again. Even now, a tug on my midsection, a warming of my thighs betrayed my answer to Redford. I wanted him so badly it hurt. If only everything I held dear—everything I wanted to be—wasn't at stake. If I gave in to my desires this time, it could be a mistake I'd never recover from.

Desperate for a distraction from my relentless thoughts of Redford who was at this moment with his buddy Jim and probably picking up women with a mere eye-twitch, I turned to the most un-sexy chore I could think of: I delved into the depths of my archived files and pulled out our tax records.

What I found was not comforting. Although I had receipts for most of the home office deductions I'd taken, the expenses themselves were a stretch—and significant. The U.S. tax code at the time was such that as a couple, we actually paid more taxes than if we had been two single people filing. I'd filled out the forms a few days before the annulment had been finalized and, in hindsight, had not been in the best frame of mind. My marriage had been a big mistake—being penalized by the government had only added salt to my wounds. I'd felt entitled to…fudge a little on the return. Now I just felt like eating fudge.

Damn, I wished I'd bought that bag of peanut M&M's.

Even worse than my questionable deductions, I'd dragged Redford into this mess. And I would be humiliated when the tax agent dressed me down for taking advantage of the government, then levied fines and penalties—maybe even criminal charges. Somehow I couldn't bear the thought of looking inept in front of him. Being dragged off in leg irons didn't hold much appeal, either.

Buried near the financial papers from the time we'd been married, I found pamphlets and books on Thoroughbreds and the Marine Corps and logistics— Redford's field of expertise in the Corps. I'd bought them at a bookstore at the Las Vegas airport to learn more about my new husband and his life—what I thought would become my life. The books were dogeared. As I flipped through, I found myself absorbed once again, as I had been three years ago, and settled against the headboard of my bed.

Logistics, I realized, had prepared Redford to run just about any kind of organization. It was good training for the Thoroughbred business he loved, which, I learned from yet another book, required managerial knowledge of every aspect of the business—from hiring good people, to buying quality stock, to overseeing the intricacies of breeding. And I do mean intricacies. Those chapters I read twice, alternately wide-eyed and wincing. Yikes. (But I still wanted to see a stallion's penis.)

Around 10:30 p.m. the phone rang. I tore myself away from my reading long enough to pick up the handset, expecting to hear Barry's voice on the other end. I couldn't wait to tell him about the tickets to Vegas.

"Hello?"

"Hi, Denise. It's Redford."

My throat closed. In the background I could hear bar noise—music, muffled voices.

"Did I catch you at a bad time?"

I guiltily set aside the book on Thoroughbreds. "Just reading. Are you and Jim having a good time?"

"Oh, yeah, sure, it's great to catch up." He cleared his throat. "Denise…I just wanted to call and say…"

"Yes?" My breath caught in my throat. Curled up in bed with the voice of a sexy guy in my ear…. Heaven help me, I felt as if I were sixteen again. My breasts grew taut beneath my thin nightshirt.

"I just wanted to say that it was great to see you again, and…well, good night."

"Good night," I murmured. "I'll see you in the morning, Redford."

"You don't know how good that sounds," he said, his voice low and earnest. "Good night, Denise."

I hung up the phone, lay my head back and groaned. Shivers skated over my skin and heat radiated from the juncture of my thighs. I was in a bad place if Redford was able to turn me on with a few innocent words.

I smoothed a hand over my stomach, then under the elastic band of my panties, closing in on the center of my pleasure. Releasing myself was insurance, I told myself. It would help me to resist the barrage of sexual cues that Redford emitted naturally...

I closed my eyes and his face came into my mind, his eyes hooded and his jaw clenched in restraint. He was above me, inside of me, thrusting cautiously at first, until I could accommodate the amazing length of him fully. Then I took over the rhythm, lifting my hips to meet him thrust for thrust. A warm hum droned deep inside me, flowing over my stomach and down to my knees. The pleasure was singular and intense. I reached under my nightshirt to stroke a budded nipple. Redford loved it when I touched myself. I groaned and strained harder against the pressure in my nest. The vibration inside intensified, like a chant of many voices, rising to the pinnacle note. The bed beneath me seemed to fall away in pieces as I shot into space, crying out his name. "Redford...Redford...ohhhhh...oohhhh...."

I lay still for a few seconds, imbedded in my mattress, marinating in the pleasurable pulsing of recovery and the languid angles of my limbs. It was the last time, I promised myself—the last time I would fantasize about being with another man…about being with Redford. I couldn't continue to condition my body to respond to him physically…his memory had become a sexual habit, I realized…one I had to break if I were ever to get on with my life.

The more my mind swirled, the more alert I became. Other worries began to infringe: the IRS audit, Ellen Brant's business, deceiving Barry and my parents, the wedding dress I was trying to win back. I tried to relax, to tell myself that I needed to be refreshed and emotionally tough to get through the next few days. Yet as I stared at the ceiling, adrenaline coursing through my veins, I knew that tonight I would get about as much sleep as I used to when Redford had been in bed with me—little to none.

_11_

Saturday
Days left on eBay auction: 3
Bidding on wedding dress up to: $1029
Winning bidder: SYLVIESMOM

THE NEXT MORNING, dead tired and running fifteen
minutes late, I trotted into the lobby of the hotel
where Redford was staying. That darned SYLVIES-
MOM seemed determined to get my dress!

Redford was leaning against a stalwart wood column, dressed in jeans and a navy blue sweatshirt,
holding his duster coat over his arm and his black hat
against his thigh. I bit back a groan—the man was
gorgeous. My stomach quickened, the memory of
last night's self-gratification fresh.

He grinned as I approached, then squinted. "Hey,
there. Are you feeling okay?"

So much for concealing my dark circles. I nodded
and fingered back a lock of hair that had fallen out
from under my wool hat. "Fine. Sorry I'm late."

"No problem," he said, nodding toward a picture

window with a particularly nice view. "I was just enjoying the scenery."

As were the people around him, I noted wryly—several women behind the reservations desk ogled him openly. I frowned, knowing that I'd probably worn that same pathetic look on my face around Redford.

"Ready to go?" I asked.

"Wherever you want to take me," he said, swinging into his coat and planting his hat on his head.

I refused to acknowledge the spike in my pulse, resolute to be the pleasant but distant tour guide. We would be so busy today, there would be no time for intimate eye contact or waxing nostalgic about our few days in Vegas. I walked two steps in front of him, pumping my arms as fast as my bulky coat would allow. I had dressed for minimum exposure and sex appeal today: loose jeans, turtleneck, chunky sweater, Merrill loafers, unflattering hat.

"I like your hat," he said, easily catching up with me with his long stride and holding open the door that led outside.

"Thanks," I murmured, bracing myself against the cold blast of February air. "I thought we'd go to the Statue of Liberty first."

"Sounds great."

"Is there anything special you'd like to see today?"

He made a rueful noise. "Ground Zero."

I stopped, my heart in my throat as I looked up at him. Of course he'd want to see the World Trade

Center site—the remnants of the event that had precipitated the U.S. re-involvement in the Gulf, where he'd spend the better part of two years, witnessing war and its aftermath.

Beneath the brim of his hat, his eyes were grave, his expression solemn. "I think it's probably necessary that I see it."

I nodded, blinking away sudden moisture, then resumed walking. "Of course," I said when I found my voice. "In fact, you'll get your first view from the ferry on the way to Liberty Island."

"Do you want me to drive?" he asked, hooking his thumb toward the hotel parking garage.

"I thought we'd take the subway."

"Great. I always wanted to ride the New York subway."

I smiled. "It'll be packed because it's Saturday, but that's part of the charm."

"If you say so," he said cheerfully.

I picked up the pace, heading toward the nearest station. "Did you have a good time last night with Jim?"

"Oh, sure," he said. "Drank a few brews. Talked about the Corps. Oh, and he gave me tickets to *42nd Street* for tonight. Want to go? We could have an early dinner."

I balked.

"Never mind," he said quickly. "You've probably seen it a dozen times."

"Actually...no." It was one of those classic Broadway shows that I just hadn't gotten around to seeing, in favor of more trendy fare. "I'd like to go."

He grinned. "Good. I really didn't want to have to ask Jim to go to a Broadway show with me."

I laughed. "Did he retire from the Corps, as well?"

"No, he's a reservist. Was called up to serve a few months, and we wound up in the same place for a while."

During the time Redford had returned from Vegas, a newly married man. I wet my lips that were already chapped from the cold, and descended stairs into the subway station.

"How has it been for you? Retirement, I mean. And...re-entry."

He smiled. "Back into civilian life, you mean? I'm adjusting. In peace time, being a career military man probably isn't so different from having a corporate job. I had regular office hours with people reporting to me and people I was accountable to. Wartime is a different animal. But it was satisfying to know that I could help my country, my fellow soldiers, my men."

"When did you come back to the States?" I asked. "Weren't you stationed in North Carolina?"

"Right. Cherry Point. But when I came back from the Gulf a year and half ago, they sent me to Albany to finish my service until retirement."

I swallowed hard. "Albany...New York?"

"Yeah. There's a Marine Logistics Base in Albany."

I averted my gaze and concentrated on buying

tickets for the train, but Redford quickly stepped up to pay. Standing behind him, waves of anguish and shock washed over me. If I'd known he'd been so close for so long…

I gave myself a mental shake. What? What would I have done? Called him up to see if we could rekindle the flame? Obviously he'd had the chance to contact me and hadn't. And why would he? I'd made it clear that we had no future together. A fact that was still true…

I chose my words carefully. "And you didn't make it to Manhattan all the time you lived in Albany?"

"Nope," he said, turning to hand me a ticket. "I was working on a special project and had very little free time. And, to be honest, the city didn't have much appeal to me at the time."

Ouch. I'd asked for that. I walked through the turnstile and found a place to stand on the platform, Redford following close behind. "We're going south to Battery Park," I said woodenly. "We'll get the ferry from there to Liberty Island."

Redford seemed fascinated by the crush of people around us…and cautious. When one of a trio of guys horsing around banged into me, Redford pulled me toward him protectively, admonishing the men.

"Watch your step."

The biggest of the three squinted at Redford, instantly belligerent. "Why don't you make me, *cowboy?*"

Alarm gripped me. "Redford—"

"Look here, son," Redford said with a smile to the man who looked to be about the same age. "Neither one of us want trouble."

The man leaned forward, thrusting his face close to Redford's. "Maybe I do—*unnnhhhh.*"

Before the thug could finish his sentence, Redford's hand had snaked out to grab the man by the neck, his thumb pressed into the man's Adam's apple. The guy emitted feeble, hissing sounds as his two cronies backed away. My heart beat wildly.

"Now I'm going to ask you again," Redford said mildly, neither his voice nor his body betraying the least amount of strain. "Watch your step. Okay, friend?" He released the troublemaker with a slight shove backward. The man grabbed his throat, gasping for air and hacking uncontrollably before disappearing into the crowd.

Oblivious to the admiring stares directed his way, Redford glanced toward the approaching train. "Is this one ours?"

"Um, yes." My eyes were still wide as the train slowed and stopped.

"You okay?"

"Redford," I said as I crowded onto the train. "That man—thank you for standing up for me, but…"

He stepped in behind me and reached up to grab a strap, effectively encircling me with his body. He raised an eyebrow. "But?"

I sighed, resisting the urge to sink against his big

body. "But you have to be careful in Manhattan. What if that guy had had a knife, or a gun? Which he probably did, by the way."

Redford seemed unfazed. "He's just a petty punk, Denise. Besides, I've been shot at lots of times."

When the train took off, my heart was still clicking in amazement and—I must admit—pride. And God help me, Redford's calm command of the situation ignited a sensual fire in me. Here was a man who would sacrifice his life for a noble cause…or for *me*.

You gotta love a man like that.

Not that I *loved* Redford. I was being hypothetical.

The train lurched forward, slamming me into Redford's chest. He steadied me with his free hand, emitting a little laugh. I looked around for a pole to grab on to, but the nearest one was filled with hands.

"Hook a finger through my belt loop," he offered.

I didn't *want* to look at his belt loop area, but after that invitation, how could I not? I lowered my gaze along the opening in his coat to take in his belt loops—and lower still, where I hadn't dared to look before. The substantial bulge I remembered was still there. (Redford, as a man's tailor would say, dressed "left.") Ignoring the stab of desire that hit me unexpectedly, I glibly hooked my pinkie through a belt loop and looked elsewhere. "Thanks."

"No, thank *you*," he said, his eyes dancing.

The ensuing flush kept me warm until we arrived at Battery Park. We made our way along the waterfront to purchase ferry tickets, then bought a cup of strong coffee and watched a woman juggle frying pans until the ferry arrived. Crowds were light because the weather was brisk. But it was a beautiful, clear, sunny day. As the ferry took off across the water, I felt as if I were in a romantic movie, standing at the rail next to a big, handsome guy, the wind blowing in my face. It would have been perfect if we had been in love. Those pesky regrets threatened to break through my careful resolve.

As we passed southern Manhattan, I pointed to the skyline and tried to explain where the twin towers had once stood. "Almost twice as tall as any building you see there."

He stared hard. "I can envision it from all the pictures I've seen." Then he pivoted his head to look at me. "You love living in the city, don't you?"

I nodded.

"Could you ever see yourself living anywhere else?"

I squirmed, remembering that once I'd naively thought I could live in Kentucky on a horse farm. I tried to make light of his question. "Well, my parents are always hinting that I move closer to them in Florida, but I've resisted."

"They're still in Fort Myers?"

I nodded, surprised that he remembered. "Are your parents still in good health?"

He smiled wide. "Oh, yeah. My mom is as sassy as ever, my dad just happy to have me back in the business. He's pushing me to expand the stables in a big way."

"I thought you were retired," I teased.

He laughed. "DeMoss men don't retire…we die in a full sweat."

I had seen Redford in a full sweat, and it *was* to die for. "A-aren't your siblings still involved in the business?"

"Both my brothers and both my sisters, and they're good. So good that I don't feel very useful most of the time."

His brothers were older, I remembered, his sisters younger. "Which one has the little girls?" I asked, although I felt as if I was prying.

"My brothers are both single," he said. "One of my sisters is married now—Sarah. She's the one with the little girls—Janie and Maggie."

I resisted the urge to ask more questions about his family. I didn't need to know. With a start, I wondered how much—if anything—they knew about me. "Do they know why you're up here?"

He nodded, but said nothing, which made me even more uncomfortable. Had Redford, like me, neglected to mention to his family that he'd gotten married in a quickie ceremony in Vegas? And if he had mentioned it, what must they think of me? My behavior must have seemed even more unwholesome to people who undoubtedly held very traditional values—not unlike my folks. My face burned.

"Oh, wow," he breathed as the Statue of Liberty came into full view.

I turned to take in the view I never tired of, no

matter how many visiting friends and relatives I brought on this trip. Newly renovated, Lady Liberty was spectacular in the morning sun—her copper robe in green and blue patinas that shimmered in the light, giving the illusion of moving cloth.

"Did you bring a camera?" I asked.

He shook his head. "I have a photographic memory." He swung his head toward me and gave me one of those intense looks. "I remember *every*thing."

My tongue adhered to the roof of my mouth. How was it possible to get turned on through a thousand layers of clothing? I maintained a frozen smile while we docked and disembarked. We bought tickets for the "insider's view," and were assigned to a park ranger for our guided tour. I hadn't visited the monument since it had been refurbished—the lighting had been enhanced and a new video system installed. But most of the time, I looked at Redford.

He listened intently as the guide explained the Statue's symbolism, history, construction, and restoration. He even asked a couple of questions. I marveled at how content I was doing something so mundane with Redford, but his sincere interest in small details made the outing more interesting to me, too.

The tour culminated in a walk out onto the statue's narrow observation deck, sixteen stories up, around the calf of Lady Liberty. From there we had a breathtaking view of New York City and the Harbor. I had a breathtaking view of Redford, too. The wind tousling his hat-flattened hair, his profile sharp and strong, his shoulders mountainous. The sheer strength that emanated from him was…inspiring. He looked over at me and winked, and I glanced away lest he think I was staring at him.

But the moment left me with a bad feeling in my stomach, as if I could be…might be…falling under his spell again. But that, I knew in my heart of hearts, would be the ruin of me. The one thing that kept me from turning around to run was the knowledge that Redford wouldn't entice me to cheat on Barry. As long as I kept my head, I'd be fine.

I repeated the mantra to myself all afternoon as we traipsed from one tourist destination to another. We ate hot dogs on the steps of the Metropolitan Museum, and Redford bought souvenirs for his nieces. We strolled through Central Park, and talked about current events and music. He asked about my job, and where I lived. The mood was light and conversational until we visited Ground Zero.

I had been to the World Trade Center site many times, but not recently…and not with anyone who seemed as connected to the site as Redford. He removed his hat as we stared over the sixteen-acre crater, bustling with construction activity in the distance, but almost silent where we stood with others who came to pay their respects. The heavy gratelike fence that surrounded the site might have been impersonal, except that portions of the fence had been turned into makeshift memorials—pictures, flowers, stuffed animals, and other items commemorating loved ones.

The temperature seemed even colder here, the wind more bitter, wailing mournfully around us.

We didn't speak. As I watched emotions play over Redford's face, my chest and throat grew tight. When he reached down to clasp my gloved hand, I didn't mind—it seemed like a moment to be touching another person. When we left the site, he still clasped my hand, and it struck me that anyone passing by would have mistaken us for a couple. And since I was engaged to another man, that didn't seem quite right.

I broke our handclasp to glance at my watch. "I guess I'd better be heading home to change. If you can find your way back to the hotel, I can cut through here to my apartment."

He nodded. "I'd like to walk to your place to pick you up, if that would be okay."

He looked so…accommodating, it would be rude to say no, I decided. Besides, it wasn't as if I was going to show him my bedroom or anything crazy like that.

"Sure." We made plans to meet in an hour and I gave him directions to my building. I felt his gaze on me as I walked away, but told myself he was only concerned about my safety, which was why he'd offered to come by.

Of course I worried all the way home. What would he think of my place? And did I really want to be able to remember Redford standing in my living room?

By the time I arrived at my apartment, I was sweating under my bulky clothes. I booted up my computer and shed the layers, then sat down to check my auction. WANTSAMAN was winning with a bid of—*gulp*—$1375! I bit my lip, feeling a little guilty for stringing along SYLVIESMOM. Then I remembered the way the woman had tried to tear the dress off my back and frowned. She'd live.

The phone rang and I raced for it, hoping it was Barry. "Hello?"

"It's Kenzie. So you're finally coming to see me, huh?"

One side of my mouth slid back. "Only if you're in a better mood."

She sighed. "I'm sorry about the other day, but this thing with your ex is really weird—I'm worried about you."

I bit my lip. "Why?"

"Because, when you came back from Vegas, it was like you'd joined a cult or something. And I'm afraid you're still hung up on this guy. I'm kind of glad he's married."

"I'm not still hung up on him, and he's not married."

"Oh. Dear. Now I'm really worried."

"Don't be, Kenzie. I'm fine, really."

"Sam says Redford is a nice guy…kind of rugged?" she said, her voice questioning.

"I…guess so."

"Well, I'll be interested to meet him, but I'm more excited that you're coming up. I've already cleared out the guest room to make room for the nursery—I can't wait to tell you my ideas."

"That's nice. But do you think you and Sam can behave yourselves long enough to have company?"

Kenzie laughed. "We don't have sex twenty-four hours a day, Denise."

"That's not what I've heard."

"My hormones are so crazy I haven't felt like having sex for two days now."

"Okay, that's approaching too much information. I'll see you tomorrow."

"Will you have your cell with you?"

"Yeah, I'll call when we get close."

We said goodbye and I hung up, Kenzie's words still playing in my mind. *"When you came back from Vegas, it was like you'd joined a cult."* I frowned. What a strange analogy, but in some way fitting for what I had experienced with Redford in that short time span in Vegas. I had lost myself, turned my mind and body over to him. And I had been so heartbroken after the annulment that months had passed before I could draw a painless breath.

I pushed the disturbing thoughts from my mind while I straightened my apartment. Then I took a shower, telling myself that my raised vital signs did not mean that I was anticipating Redford's arrival.

I was in a quandary about what to wear. Chances were, Redford would be wearing jeans or chinos and maybe a dress shirt. I didn't want to appear too dressy, but I wanted to look nice. Not for Redford, but for...anyone.

Yes, I wanted to look nice not for Redford, but for perfect strangers.

I settled on a plain V-neck black dress and strappy sandals, with my standard low ponytail and simple jewelry.

I paused to study my engagement ring, and guilt consumed me. On impulse, I picked up the phone and dialed Barry's cell phone. To my surprise, he answered. It was a sign, I decided.

"Hi," I said. "Did I catch you at a bad time?"

"Just trying to wade through a month's worth of Nielsen ratings."

I pictured him on the other end rubbing his eyes. Working like a dog, while I entertained my ex. "I talked to my mom yesterday and told her about the engagement. She's thrilled. Dad, too."

"That's great," he said. "I haven't told my folks yet, haven't had a chance to call and have a conversation."

I closed my eyes. "I miss you."

"Me, too," he said. "Are you doing something fun tonight?"

"Um, maybe," I said, fingering my ring. "You?"

He laughed. "Hardly." His phone made a clicking noise. "I'm sorry, Denise, I need to get this. Can I call you tomorrow?"

I would be on the road with Redford tomorrow. "I…might be out."

"Okay, then I'll catch up with you Monday."

Then I'd tell him about the tickets to Vegas. "Sure. Bye…Barry."

"Bye."

I hung up the phone, fighting an unreasonable spike of frustration with Barry because he hadn't taken the time to reassure me that he adored me and that we were good together. When I glanced at my sparkling diamond again, though, I felt horrible. The ring spoke volumes. Hadn't he taken the time to get to know me over two years? Hadn't he gotten to know my parents and my friends? Hadn't he taken an interest in my career and hooked me up to do business with his *boss,* no less? And hadn't he gone to the trouble of buying me a fabulous ring and proposing in public? And while he wasn't a dynamo in bed, he was at least *there* in body and spirit. Redford had been living a couple of hours away for over a year and hadn't bothered to look me up.

A knock on my door sounded and I inhaled deeply. Maybe an evening at a Broadway show would convince me once and for all how different Redford and I really were: city girl, country boy. I smoothed a hand down my sleeve, hoping I wasn't overdressed, then swung open the door.

And hung on to the knob to keep from falling.

Redford stood there, hatless, looking like a million dollars in a black suit, white shirt, and black dress shoes. A taupe-colored wool scarf that looked remarkably like cashmere was draped casually around his neck. His dark hair was neatly combed, still slightly damp, his square jaw clean-shaven. In a word, he was…mouthwatering. (Or was that two words?)

"You look beautiful," he said.

I finally found my voice. "You look…great…too."

His grin was the perfect accessory. "Do I pass?"

"Um…yes."

"Good. I wouldn't want you to be embarrassed to be seen with me."

I swallowed. "No chance of that." I gestured behind me. "Just let me get my coat."

And my resolve, I thought as he followed me inside.

12

REDFORD STEPPED INSIDE my apartment and closed the door behind him. "Nice place," he said, nodding.

I tried to picture the eclectic furniture and scarred wood floors from his perspective. "It's old," I said with a little smile. "But it's solid and the neighbors aren't psychopaths." I pointed. "Living room here, kitchen there, study there, bathroom there, bedroom…there. It's small. Everything in New York is small." I was babbling.

"It's nice," he repeated, running his hand along a built-in wooden bookshelf. "Good bones, lots of character. Did you say you were going to buy it?"

I nodded. "Someday." As soon as Ellen Brant opened her account and my commission check was cut.

"So you and your fiancé are going to live here?"

I blinked. "Well…I don't know." The truth was, I hadn't even thought about it. Barry and I had lived separately—and contentedly—for so long, I just assumed… Frankly, I don't know what I assumed.

He accepted my ambiguous answer and studied the framed photographs on the bookshelf. "These must be your parents."

I nodded. "In front of their home in Florida."

"You look like your mother."

I warmed because I thought my mother was beautiful. "Thank you."

"Who are these people?" he asked, gesturing to other frames.

"My girlfriends," I said. "There's Jacki and her husband Ted. There's Cindy." I smiled. "She's single, but determined to meet Mr. Right. And this is Kenzie, Sam's wife."

"I'll meet her tomorrow."

"Right," I said slowly, thinking ahead to the long drive. "I thought I'd bring our tax files and we could discuss the audit."

He looked uncomfortable, then recovered. "Sure."

But his reaction made me think that he was dreading the audit more than he let on. No doubt he was worried about the potential cash outlay…as was I. Not to mention the exposure of my tax-cheating ways.

"And this must be your boyfriend?"

My head jerked around to look at the small frame of Barry, his corporate head shot. "Fiancé. And, yes, that's….him."

"Nice-looking fellow."

Thanking him seemed weird, so I just smiled and headed toward the closet to get my coat.

"Does he smoke cigars?"

"Hmm?" I pulled out my coat, turned my head and froze. The Punch cigar box of keepsakes from our wedding sat on the shelf. Redford tapped it with his finger. I didn't want him to know what a sentimental fool I was. "No!" I practically shouted, and he jerked back his hand.

"I'm sorry, I didn't mean to pry."

I felt ridiculous. "No, it's okay, really. I…" My voice petered out and I stood there, stewing in my deceit. I wondered idly if I was losing my mind. Some people say it's always the quiet ones that will fool a person, and I decided that was me. On the surface, I was a nice, thrifty, hardworking good girl. But deep down, I was naughty.

I had begun the train of thought half in jest, but by the end, the revelation that I wasn't a very good person struck me hard…was it possible that the hedonistic, hypersexual, irresponsible way I'd behaved with Redford in Vegas was the true Denise Cooke, and the rest of this was just an act?

"Are you okay?" Redford asked, taking my coat and holding it behind me. "You look like something hurts."

I pressed my lips together, then shook my head. "Just hungry, I suppose."

"I can fix that. Ready to go?"

I nodded and followed him outside into the cold and down the sidewalk, in the direction of a more well-traveled street in order to catch a cab.

"Nice neighborhood," he said.

"Yes. It'll be beautiful in the spring." I dug my gloved hands deeper into my pockets. "Everything really comes alive."

"Sorry I'll miss it," he said with a wistful note in his voice.

I looked over at him. "I'll bet Kentucky is beautiful in the spring, too."

"Oh, sure—nothing like it."

"Is the grass really blue?"

He laughed. "Sometimes. Actually, bluegrass is a type of grass that has a dark cast to it. When it's tall and blowing in the fields, it looks blue."

When we got to the curb, he surprised me by hailing a cab like a pro. I slid inside, saying, "There are lots of good places to eat close to the theater. We shouldn't have a problem—"

"I made reservations," he cut in.

"Oh…that's nice."

"The concierge at the hotel recommended a place called Millweed's."

The place where Barry had proposed. My throat constricted. "Yes, I've…heard of it."

"Is that okay with you?"

"It's great," I said cheerfully. In fact, what better place to be reminded of Barry?

The restaurant hadn't changed much in the six days since I'd been there, except for the addition of a piano player. As luck would have it, we were seated at the same table where Barry and I had been seated. I wasn't surprised—in fact, I rather expected it. When the same waiter appeared, a strange sense of déjà vu enveloped me. It was as if some otherworldly power was forcing me to compare the two men—one I had a life with, the other I had a lust with.

"Okay, I get it," I murmured to myself.

"Pardon me?" Redford said, one eyebrow raised.

"I said I think I'll get a glass of wine."

"How about a bottle?"

"Even better."

The waiter was staring at me. "Weren't you...?"

He remembered me. I shifted in my seat and tried to look clueless. He glanced at Redford and back to me and cleared his throat. "Never mind."

Redford looked at me and I shrugged. After surveying the wine menu, he ordered a bottle of something I'd never heard of that seemed to impress the waiter. I was accustomed to Redford in his hat and boots, drinking a long-neck beer. I was comfortable with the *aw-shucks* version. This refined side of Redford disarmed me. The man sitting across from me would have looked at home at the head of any corporate boardroom.

And was so achingly handsome that he would be welcome in any woman's *bed*room.

"Does your ring need to be sized?" Redford asked.

I blinked. "Pardon me?"

He pointed to my left hand. "You keep twisting your ring."

I looked down to see that he was right. "Um, maybe I do need to get it cut down a bit."

"Size six, right?"

I nodded, surprised that he remembered, although

anything he did at this point shouldn't have surprised me. I clenched my hands together in my lap, grateful when the waiter reappeared to present the bottle of wine to Redford. He glanced at the label and nodded, then the waiter uncorked the bottle and poured a half-inch into his glass. I watched, mesmerized, as Redford held up his glass to look at the brilliantly berry-hued wine. Then he swirled the liquid slightly and inhaled the aroma before taking a sip and nodding to the waiter. "Very good."

The waiter filled my glass, then Redford's glass, and took our orders—steak for Redford, trout for me. When we were left alone, I felt trapped. I wanted to stare at Redford, to drink him in, yet I didn't dare. To avoid eye contact, I sipped my wine…heartily. Whether Redford picked up on my discomfort or was feeling uneasy himself, I wasn't sure, but he seemed content to listen to the pianist and empty his own glass. Gradually, I relaxed, even closing my eyes.

"Would you like to dance?" Redford asked.

My eyes popped open. "Dance?"

"You know—stand close and move our feet at the same time, more or less."

I gave a little laugh. "I…don't know."

"Come on," he said, standing and extending his hand. "I don't get dressed up that often."

I stared at his hand and in one split second, I recalled the magic that those long, blunt fingers had worked on my body. Of its own accord, my hand went into his and I felt myself being pulled to my feet. I followed Redford the short distance to the tiny, dimly-lit dance floor next to the piano and told myself it was safe for us to touch in front of so many people.

He pulled me close in a slow, smooth waltz—my right hand in his left, near his shoulder, his other hand firmly on my lower back. My left hand I laid loosely on his shoulder, keeping my engagement ring in sight. Redford moved with remarkable grace and natural athleticism. Beneath my hand, I felt the muscles move in his shoulder, felt the heat radiate from his body. He had taken me dancing in Vegas, I recalled, and had held me so close we had breathed the same air. I looked up into his face, my heart buoyed crazily by the glimmer in his dark eyes.

Wordlessly, we found a rhythm and our bodies moved in tandem. My breasts brushed the wall of his chest and I closed my eyes against the thrill that zinged through my body. And to shut out the glimmer of my ring.

Our bodies merged as close as public decency laws would allow. I put my cheek against his shoulder and drew the clean, minty scent of him into my lungs. He put his chin next to my temple and I imagined that he pressed his lips against my skin. *What-ifs* revolved in my head while my body responded to distant memories…sexual familiarity.

Suddenly I became aware of the hardening of

his sex against my stomach. He retreated from me slightly, but knowing how I affected him made me feel heady. I followed him and brushed against the length of his erection with the slightest twist of my body. I felt his jaw clench and he emitted a low groan.

"Don't start something you don't intend to finish."

Tiny hairs raised on the back of my neck, and I shivered. Being in Redford's arms intercepted all rational signals to my brain. Feeling like a tease, I stepped back and inhaled deeply. A glance at our table showed our food had been delivered, topped with warming covers. "We should eat—we don't want to be late for the show."

He nodded curtly, visibly straining—willing away his hard-on, no doubt. I tried to help by walking back to the table slowly and in front of him. When we arrived at the table, he held out my chair. I sat, still tingling from our encounter. After scooting my chair in, he leaned down and murmured, "That was close."

A thought I repeated to myself throughout our dinner and the show; but as the evening progressed, it was harder and harder to remember why being close to Redford was so treacherous. Our seats for *42nd Street* were spectacular and the show itself was amazing— quintessential Broadway. Coupled with the fact that people around us stared at Redford. "Is he a movie star?" someone behind us whispered. And all I could think was how much I enjoyed his company. He laughed and applauded throughout the show, occasionally looking over to wink or smile. When the show was over, heaven help me, I didn't want to go home.

As we walked through the lobby, I cleared my throat. "Redford, I was thinking…since we didn't make it to the Empire State Building today, what would you think about going…now?"

"Is it open late?"

"Until midnight. The city is beautiful at night."

He grinned. "Sounds great. I'll get our coats."

I stood there watching him walk away, and my insides welled with anticipation…and trepidation. This reunion with Redford wasn't going as I'd planned. Instead of remembering all the logical reasons I had for ending the marriage, I was remembering all the titillating reasons why I'd said, "I do" in the first place.

"Denise? Oh, it *is* you."

At the sound of my name, I turned…and froze. Barry's boss Ellen Brant was coming toward me, all smiles.

13

As Ellen walked toward me, I slid my gaze across the room toward Redford, who was handing the clerk our coat-check tickets. A sweat broke out along my hairline, but I managed a smile for Ellen and the older woman next to her. "Hi, Ellen. Did you enjoy the show?"

She gave a dismissive wave. "I've seen *42nd Street* a dozen times, but Mother can't get enough of it."

She introduced me to her mother. I nodded politely, eager to disappear. "It was nice to meet you—"

"Denise is newly engaged to one of the station's producers," Ellen told her mother. "I believe you've met Barry Copeland?"

Her mother nodded. "I met Barry at the station once. He's a handsome young man. Congratulations on your engagement."

I smiled, near panic. "Thank you."

"I'm looking forward to getting together Tuesday afternoon," Ellen said with a little society laugh. "I've got to get my ex-husband's money working for me as soon as possible."

I tried to chuckle, but it sounded more like a hiccup. "You'll feel good about working with Trayser Brothers."

"I feel good about working with *you,* Denise," Ellen said magnanimously. "A person can't trust their money to just anyone these days."

"How true. I don't mean to be short, but—"

"Here you go," Redford said, holding my coat behind me.

Dead silence fell around us. I gave him a tight smile and slid my arms inside, my heart thudding in my ears. I dreaded lifting my gaze; when I did, as expected, Ellen's mother was frowning quizzically at Redford, and Ellen's penciled eyebrows had climbed high on her forehead.

My mind swirled. If I introduced them, word would get back to Barry. If I didn't, word would *definitely* get back to Barry, and on top of that, Ellen would probably write me off for being rude. I cleared my throat.

"This is Ellen Brant, the general manager of a local television network, and her mother. Ladies, this is, um…um…"

"Her neighbor," Redford cut in and his voice had taken on a…*feminine* edge?

I swung my gaze to him, baffled.

He reached forward and shook the women's hands with two fingers, his wrist as limp as a dishrag. "How do you do? *Love* those earrings."

"Thank you," Ellen said, rearranging her face

from suspicion into a knowing smile. "Did you enjoy the show?"

"Oh, did I! It gets better *every* time," he said, clasping his hands together, a wistful expression on his face.

My mind could not comprehend what I was seeing and hearing. Redford DeMoss, career military man and the most heterosexual man I'd ever met, pretending to be…*gay?* I was stupefied.

"Well, it was nice meeting you," Ellen said to Redford. "Denise, I'll see you Tuesday afternoon." Then she leaned forward and sighed near my ear. "All the best-looking men are gay, aren't they?"

I nodded and made sympathetic noises and wished them well. Only when they had disappeared from sight could I bring myself to look at Redford, who wore an innocent expression.

"*What* was that?" I asked, crossing my arms.

"What?"

"That bad impression of Steven Cojocaru."

"Who?"

"A TV personality. He's…flamboyant."

Redford shrugged. "Just trying to help you out of a spot. You said the woman worked for a television station. I assume she knows your boyfriend?"

"Fiancé," I corrected. "Ellen is his boss."

He lifted his hands. "So…you're welcome."

My face burned when I realized why he'd done what he'd done. So word wouldn't get back to Barry that I was out with another man—another *straight* man. "Thank you, Redford."

He pressed his lips together. "I just hope he deserves you."

I couldn't speak. Deserve *me?* I was doing things behind Barry's back. *He* deserved someone better than me. I glanced down and rubbed a finger over my engagement ring.

Redford sighed heavily. "But if you tell anyone what I did, I'll have to kill you."

I looked up and laughed, shaking my head. "All gay men don't act that over-the-top."

He shrugged. "I know, but I improvised. It worked, didn't it?"

I pursed my mouth, then nodded.

He looked at me, then fingered a lock of my hair that had come loose from my ponytail, leaving a tingling trail across my skin. "You promised me a night view from the top of the Empire State Building."

I exhaled and smiled. "Yes, I did."

The Empire State Building was always a crowded attraction, but at this time of the day there were fewer children. And at this time of the year, people stayed on the observatory for less time, so the lines moved quickly. When we stepped out onto the observatory, I shivered in my coat—the air temperature at this height was breathtaking. Redford saw my reaction and put his arm around me. I didn't object—I couldn't imagine any mischief unfolding in the frigid air and blustery wind.

Redford was immediately riveted to the unending view—lights twinkling and moving across the city like Christmas tree decorations, buildings glowing as if they were atop a Lite-Brite board. I pointed out landmarks as we walked all around the platform—the George Washington Bridge, the Chrysler Building, Times Square, the Reuters Building, the Woolworth Building.

"It's like being on top of the world," Redford said.

I nodded, then broached a subject that had been eating at me. "Redford, are you…seeing someone special back in Kentucky?"

He shook his head then looked back to the view. "No."

I wet my parched lips. "Are women scarce in Kentucky?"

He laughed. "Not at all."

Which meant he looked…as any normal red-blooded single man would do. I injected a teasing note into my voice. "I would think that you could have just about any woman you wanted."

His laugh was self-deprecating, but he didn't offer a comment. For my part, I wished I hadn't asked. Redford's love life was none of my business…anymore.

A bitter gust of wind blasted us, and my teeth began to chatter. Redford pulled me in front of him and shielded me with his big body, rubbing my arms briskly with his hands. Suddenly his hands slowed and a few seconds later, he lowered his arms and crossed them over my chest. I felt his chest rise and fall with a sigh. I closed my eyes and eased my head back against him, then raised my hands to cover his.

He hugged me closer against him, uttering a low moan that reverberated through my body.

"Denise," he whispered against my temple. "I—"

I didn't let him finish. I lifted my mouth to his for a desperate, jarring, upside-down kiss. His lips were warm and firm, his tongue strong and determined. I sighed into his mouth and strained against the awkward angle. He broke the kiss long enough to turn me in his arms, and I met him again, willingly.

My mouth remembered his—every texture, every flavor. Our teeth clicked and our tongues danced, sending white-hot desire shooting through me. I pushed my hands into his hair and kneaded the back of his neck, pulling his mouth closer, deeper. His arms tightened around me and even through my coat, I could feel his urgent desire for me. My body leapt in response, also remembering that magic wand of his. The way his face contorted with pleasure when he thrust deep into me…heaven…

I pressed my body against his erection and he groaned. His hands slid down my back and underneath me, pulling me against him. I gave in to the thrill of him and thrust my hands through the opening in his coat to wrap my arms around his warm back, pulling him closer. I lowered my hand to stroke the thick knob of his shaft through his clothing, and he sucked in a sharp breath.

The sound of persistent throat-clearing reached my ears—and apparently Redford's. We lifted our heads to see a security guard standing a few feet away trying to look as if he hadn't noticed us. I realized other people around us were doing their best to ignore us, and I flushed with embarrassment. Making out in public—was I sixteen years old?

"Let's go," I murmured, my ragged breath coming out in white puffs.

Redford tried to take my hand, but I pulled it back and stuffed it deep into my coat pocket. His mouth tightened, but he didn't press me. Our walk back to the elevator bay and the ride down were quiet. I assumed his mind was as chaotic as mine...or perhaps not since he didn't have as much at stake. For Redford, a weekend fling would simply be a pleasurable reunion. For me, it would be going back to a place where my body overrode my mind, and I couldn't live the rest of my life that way. I had a good, logical life waiting for me, with Barry...a man whose ring I wore, whose proposal I'd accepted mere days ago. What kind of woman was I that I could be tempted into an affair so soon after taking a man's ring?

That kind of woman...carnal...reckless...rash.

No! I would not barter my long-term happiness for short-term gratification.

When we exited the building, the wind had kicked up, howling around us, sending litter twirling in the streets and making it nearly impossible to talk. I wanted the wind to pick me up and twirl me into next week. My eBay auction would be over, the IRS audit would be over and I'd have Ellen Brant's business. My life would be back to normal...better than normal because I would be a content engaged woman with a fat bonus in the bank, and a wedding dress in my closet.

And Redford would be a memory.

His dress shoes sounded against the sidewalk with military precision, the wind whipping the legs of his slacks. At the curb Redford hailed a cab and we slid inside. I huddled against the door inside my coat, Redford staring out the window, occasionally pulling on his chin. A couple of times, he started to say something, but changed his mind. When the cabbie neared my building, I leaned forward. "Let me out at the next corner, please."

"We'll both get out," Redford said.

"You can go on to your hotel."

"I'll walk to the hotel," he said in a voice that brooked no argument.

I alighted from the cab, steeled for the argument I knew was imminent. When Redford paid the cabbie, he turned to look at me and jammed his hands on his hips. "Denise—"

"I'm sorry, Redford," I said, my voice clipped. "I made a mistake kissing you back there."

He was quiet for a few seconds. "Are you saying you don't have feelings for me?"

His question startled me in its directness. For a few seconds, I was flustered, then irritated. "Redford, how can you ask me that? I'm *engaged* to another man."

"A few minutes ago, you weren't thinking about your boyfriend."

"*Fiancé.*"

"Whatever." He stepped closer to me and tipped my chin up with his hand, forcing me to look at him. His eyes glittered in the shadow of a streetlight. "Denise, I was on the receiving end of that kiss. Do you have feelings for me?" His Adam's apple bobbed. "Did you ever?"

A lump formed in my throat and my tongue felt swollen in my mouth. "Redford, my feelings…" I swallowed and tried again. "The feelings that we…that I…had for you…when we first met." I gestured vaguely. "I was caught up in you…in your sexuality…in your openness. I confused my physical attraction for you with…love." I exhaled and brushed the hair out of my eyes. "So…yes, I'm still attracted to you…obviously. But…" I pressed my lips together.

He dropped his hand and gave a little laugh. "So I'm only good for meaningless sex."

"I didn't say that."

"It's okay, Denise." His shoulders lifted in a shrug, then he put his hands in his slacks pockets. "That's not such a bad thing for a man to hear." A sardonic smile came over his mouth. "I had a wonderful time with you today…and tonight. And if it makes you feel better, I promise to keep my open sexuality under wraps tomorrow."

I shook my head. "Redford, I don't think I should go upstate with you."

He cocked one eyebrow. "Oh, come on, I'm not *that* irresistible. Besides, I thought we were going to go over our tax files." He gave me a teasing grin. "That should pretty much kill any inclination to... make a mistake...shouldn't it?"

Standing there with his hands in his pockets and the wind ruffling his hair, he looked boyish and completely harmless. Like a rejected prom date, content to be friends. I sighed. Kenzie would be disappointed if I didn't go. And Redford and I did need to talk about our taxes. And it seemed that we *had* cleared the air of our inappropriate attraction. "Okay. What time should I be ready?"

He smiled. "I'll pick you up at eight. Bring some riding clothes."

He was striding away before his words sunk in. *Riding clothes?* He couldn't possibly mean *horse* riding clothes...although, was there another kind? "I don't like horses!" I yelled after him, but he only threw up his hand dismissively.

"I...don't...like...*horses!*" I shouted at the top of my lungs, but the wind whisked my words away.

I frowned and walked inside my apartment muttering, "I don't like horses."

14

Sunday
Days left on eBay auction: 2
Bidding on wedding dress up to: $1653
Winning bidder: SYLVIESMOM

WHEN I OPENED THE DOOR Sunday morning, Redford stood silhouetted in the early morning sunshine wearing faded jeans, a blue work shirt, a tan corduroy jacket and, of course, the hat.

So much for not being irresistible.

He gestured at my wool skirt and sweater. "Those don't look like riding clothes."

I set my jaw against an internal reaction to his outrageous sexiness, then crossed my arms. "I…don't… like…horses. You and Sam are going to look at your stud. Kenzie and I…aren't." I turned around and he followed me inside.

"Horses are the most beautiful animals that God created—well, aside from women."

I gave him a bland smile.

"At least wear some sensible shoes."

I looked down at my suede clogs. "These are sensible."

He clapped his hands together. "Okay. Ready to go?"

"I just need to get a bag of clothes I'm taking to Kenzie. Oh, and would you mind helping me with the box of tax papers sitting outside the bedroom door?"

I went into my bedroom to pick up my purse and the bag. When I checked inside the bag, I remembered with a start that I'd included the sweater Redford had given me when we'd first met. I entertained thoughts of keeping it, then told myself that getting rid of the sweater was for the best. I needed to get rid of all my Vegas keepsakes. I wasn't sure what I would do with my lovely wedding band, but eBay was always an option. The thought of selling it online gave me a queasy feeling, but it was the logical thing to do. Considering I was marrying someone else, that is.

At the sound of footsteps behind me, I turned to see Redford standing in the doorway, holding the box of papers and staring at something off to the right. I followed his line of vision and my pulse blipped. Last night I had removed my wedding gown from the closet and hung it from the mirror on my dressing table, both to get it out of the way and as an extra reminder of where my head should be.

"Wow," he said. "Nice dress. You'll be a beautiful bride, Denise."

I shifted uncomfortably. "Thanks."

His gaze was level and earnest. "I'm glad to see you plan to do it right this time."

I looked away. I had thought the same thing myself, but hearing it from Redford was unsettling.

"We have a long drive ahead of us," he said quietly. "We'd better get going. I'm parked illegally."

"Right."

We walked outside and he put the box in the back seat of the monster truck. "Wait and I'll help you up," he said across the expansive hood.

"I can do it," I said, remembering the full-body slide the last time he'd "helped" me. I grabbed a hand strap and after a couple of bounces, vaulted myself into the seat, landing with less than gymnastic precision. I closed the door with a solid bang, then fastened my seat belt and exhaled, exhausted.

Redford climbed inside, grinning, and put his hat on the seat between us. "You're getting the hang of it."

The words were on the tip of my tongue to point out that sling shotting myself into a gargantuan truck was not likely to be a skill that I would use again, but I realized he was only making conversation. I was being too sensitive…too vulnerable. And the day had just begun.

He started the engine and maneuvered the vehicle out of its spot and down the narrow side street, watching both mirrors to make sure he didn't clip something or somebody.

"Do you really need this big of a truck?" I asked.

"Yeah, to pull horse trailers. The double cab is a

luxury, though. It's nice to have room for extra supplies or extra people."

I laughed. "I can't believe how much it cost."

"Jim gave me a great deal—we worked it out over the phone."

So he hadn't paid full sticker price. "Oh. Good."

"It's nice to have a comfortable vehicle for a long trip."

"It's comfortable," I agreed, feeling cradled in the leather seat. "Will you be on the road a lot?"

"Quite a bit during the sales season, twice a year."

I smiled. "You'd think you'd have a cell phone."

He pursed his mouth. "No. Don't see much need for one. Have you had breakfast?"

I shook my head. "I'm not hungry, but coffee sounds good."

"I was thinking the same thing."

He pulled up to a drive-through and got two steaming cups to go. Before pulling back out on the street, he reached under the seat and withdrew an atlas. "Do you want to navigate?"

I sipped from my cup and murmured with pleasure as the warm liquid slid down my throat. "Sure."

"Care if I turn on some music?"

"No. That would be nice."

He found a country music station—which I didn't even know existed within the vicinity of the city—and turned it to a pleasing volume. Soon we were on our way to the interstate and I looked around, suddenly struck by the surreal scene: I was in a truck with my ex on a horse-buying road trip, listening to country music. He sat behind the wheel, completely at ease. And why not? This was his life. And this would have been my life if I'd stayed married to Redford.

"You okay?" he asked, shifting in his seat. The muscles in his legs rippled beneath the fabric of his jeans, diverting my attention…and my concentration. "Are you warm enough?"

Was I ever. I nodded, then looked out the window, taking in the passing landscape. I'd never been north of the city, so all the road signs and landmarks were alien to me. I smiled, thinking about Kenzie making this fateful trip to see Sam Long under the guise of doing an article on the small-town hero. Kenzie was even more of a city girl than I was, and had been hoodwinked into taking her boss's dog with her. But the trip had changed the trajectory of her life.

I glanced at Redford under my lashes and thought about how my life had changed when I'd met him. Within a few hours, my entire persona had seemed to change—I had turned into a lust-crazed creature with no regard for the ramifications of my actions.

Good God. In hindsight, I had morphed into a man.

I turned my attention back to the scenery racing by, and Redford seemed content to do the same. On the one hand, I was glad not to talk, but on the other, I was disturbed, frankly, over how comfortable we were not talking.

I was a mess.

Fairly quickly, Manhattan fell away behind us and the traffic thinned. An hour into the projected four-hour drive, we were traveling on a two-lane road lined with frost-encrusted trees and sudden small towns. Redford occasionally leaned forward to glance at the sky, his brow furrowed.

"Is something wrong?" I asked.

"It's clouding up," he said. "The forecast said snow tomorrow, so let's hope it holds off."

"Right," I said with a little laugh. "I would hate to get snowed in."

"I could think of worse things," he said, slanting a smile in my direction.

My breasts tingled. "Redford," I chided.

"I just meant we'd have a good excuse to miss the IRS audit," he said, trying to sound indignant. "What did you think I meant?"

I gave him a stern frown. "Never mind. But that reminds me—" I turned around to lift the lid from the box containing our tax papers. "I had a chance to go over the forms, and there are a few things we should talk about before the interview."

He sipped from his coffee cup, then winced. "Do we have to?"

"Yes."

His mouth tightened. "Okay, but I should warn you that my expertise is in logistics, not numbers." Then he grinned. "Luckily, you're great with numbers. I'm not worried. We'll probably walk out of there with a refund."

I squirmed. "I suspect they'll ask a lot of questions about the deductions I took on my home-office expenses."

He shrugged. "So, you'll just explain, that's all."

I swallowed hard. His confidence in me made me feel even worse. "Still, I'd like to go over everything so we go in looking united."

"You mean like a team?"

"Sort of." I rummaged around in the box and removed the form, which was several pages thick.

"That's our form?" he asked. "I don't remember it being that thick."

"You didn't read it before you signed it?"

"No...I trusted you."

Which certainly didn't make me feel better, considering we'd been flagged for an audit. "Okay, let's start with the numbers and how I came up with them." I switched to professional mode, launching into a discussion of the form, attached schedules, and supporting documents—which, between his complicated pay schedule and overseas status, were considerable. To his credit, his eyes didn't glaze over. But halfway through the file, and an hour later, he broke in with a little laugh.

"Gee, Denise, no wonder you wanted out of the marriage. You probably couldn't face dealing with the tax forms every year."

I couldn't think of an answer, so I didn't give him one. And just like that, I felt the mood in the cab of the truck change.

"I'm so sorry, Denise."

I turned to look at him. "For what?"

His expression was pained. "For…proposing. You barely knew me. I was on my way back to the Gulf, not sure when I'd return. It was crazy. To be honest, I was relieved when I got those annulment papers."

I had assumed as much, but hearing it was like a kick in the stomach. "There's no need to apologize, Redford. It takes two people to make that kind of mistake."

"Yeah, but you were the one smart enough to try to remedy the situation. Thanks to you, we were both able to resume our lives without any fallout. I'm grateful, Denise."

My throat constricted suddenly…and I wasn't sure why. It was exactly what I'd been hoping Redford would say someday: that he hadn't felt abandoned or angry when I'd filed for an annulment; that it was the right thing to do under the circumstances. I should have felt relieved…so why didn't I?

"There's a convenience store up ahead," he said. "By my estimation, we're halfway there. Want to stretch our legs?"

I nodded, grateful for a break. From both the confines of the truck, and our discussion.

Redford pulled up next to the gas pump—I couldn't imagine how much gasoline it took to keep the monster truck running. When I alighted, I noticed the sky was indeed growing cloudy and gray, which wasn't uncommon for February, but unsettling none-theless. I glanced at my watch and decided to wait until we were closer to call Kenzie, especially since I couldn't get a signal on my phone here.

After I exited the ladies' room, I pulled a bottle of water from a wall cooler and walked up to the counter where Redford had engaged the rotund clerk in a conversation about—as near as I could tell—fishing lures. The man could befriend anyone.

"I'll get that," Redford said, taking my water. I acquiesced, knowing it wouldn't do any good to argue, then walked outside to get as much fresh air as possible before we set off again.

I dragged the cool air into my lungs slowly, mulling over Redford's "gratitude" to me for having our marriage annulled. His admission, coupled with the knowledge that he had lived so close to me after he returned to the States, was—I had to concede—bruising my ego.

My chest ached with unexpected grief, and tears gathered on my lashes. (I never cried…*ever.*) My ego was more than bruised. To be honest, I was crushed. Which was incredibly foolish and selfish of me, considering I was the one who had ended the marriage, and I was the one who was engaged to marry again.

"Ready to hit the road?" Redford called behind me.

I blinked like mad to dissipate the tears—thankful that I could blame runny eyes and a red nose on the weather, if necessary. But when I turned, the sight of Redford standing there looking so impossibly masculine in his jeans and boots and black hat was sobering enough to evaporate any tears—along with all the moisture in my mouth. Defeated, I headed back to the truck and hurdled into my seat.

"You okay?" Redford asked when he fastened his seat belt.

"I wish you would stop asking me that," I snapped.

He blinked, then a little smile came over his face. "I know what you want."

I closed my eyes, at my wits' end with his innuendos and worse, with my Pavlovian responses. "Redford—" I stopped when I opened my eyes and saw what he had in his hand. A bag of peanut M&M's.

"These used to be your favorite."

I sighed. "They still are."

"Good." He handed me the candy, then pulled two bottles of water from the small plastic bag.

"You didn't want a snack?" I asked, tearing open the candy.

"I was hoping you'd share."

"No way," I said, laughing.

"Take them all," he said as he started the engine. "The more you have in your mouth, the less you can talk about taxes."

I stuck my tongue out at him and he laughed as he pulled the truck back onto the road. Despite his teasing, he ate a few pieces of the candy, and I was struck again by the alternate ease and discomfort I felt when I was with Redford. It was like being on a roller coaster…in the first car with nothing to hold on to…except Redford himself.

"Back to the taxes," I said when the last piece had been washed down.

"Please, no," he begged. "Tell me about your friends, Kenzie and Sam."

A legitimate question…and an interesting story. "Kenzie works for *Personality* magazine. Sam was on the cover one month for the 'small-town hero' issue. He's a veterinarian, and a part-time fireman in Jar Hollow, and he saved a lot of people in a nursing-home fire."

He pursed his mouth, nodding.

"Anyway, they met when he went to the city to have his photo taken. Then she went to his place to do a follow-up article…and then there was the cover curse."

"Cover curse?"

"It's a long story, but basically Kenzie went to stay on his farm for a while and got into all kinds of predicaments, including almost burning down his clinic."

"Yikes."

"But Sam fell in love with her anyway."

"That's a helluva guy."

"So, long story short, Sam teaches in the city a few days a week, and she works from their home up here a few days a week, so they're together as much as possible." I smirked. "I have to warn you, though— Sam and Kenzie are shmoops."

"Is that some kind of northern religion?"

I laughed. "No. I mean, they smooch and look at each other like teenagers. And Kenzie talks about how much they—" I stopped and cleared my throat as Redford fought a smile. "Anyway, the girls and I call them shmoops."

"Okay, well I'll try not to notice if their clothes start flying off."

"Now, back to the taxes…"

He groaned. "Why don't we save that for the drive home this evening?"

"I won't be able to read in the dark!"

His white teeth flashed in a wide grin. "I know."

I sighed. "Okay, there isn't much left anyway. For the most part, I…I just need to make sure that Tuesday morning we go in there—"

"United," he finished. "Got it. They will see one united couple, by golly. We'll be so united, they'll think we're still married."

"Well," I murmured, settling back in my seat, "we don't have to take it that far."

I tried to call Kenzie several times on my cell phone, but couldn't get a signal, and then when I did, my battery was dead. But Sam's directions were good and, after passing through the adorably quaint town of Jar Hollow, (I saw some of the businesses that Kenzie had mentioned to me—the Cut and Curl, Jamison Hardware Store), and driving up a steep hill, we pulled into a clearing that gave way to a plateau with a picturesque view that would be stunning in the spring. I could see why Kenzie would have been enchanted.

From her description, I recognized a smaller log building, which would be the clinic, to the right of where we sat; and the larger building, the log home that Sam had built himself, to the left. It was spectacular.

"Nice," Redford murmured. He nodded toward the two vehicles—Sam's truck and Kenzie's car. "Looks like they're home."

I opened the door and climbed down. "They probably heard us pull up."

Redford put on his hat and together we walked to the front of the cabin. The picture-perfect landscaping was undoubtedly Kenzie's handiwork. I rang the doorbell and from inside, a horrific noise erupted—like a dog pound on the night of a full moon.

"That would be their pets," I explained.

"Good watchdogs," Redford said.

When a few seconds passed and no one came to the door, I said, "Maybe they're at the clinic."

"Or maybe they're…you know." Redford's eyebrows wagged suggestively.

I smirked. "I forgot to tell you that Kenzie's pregnant."

He laughed. "Big surprise."

"I mean, she said that lately she hasn't been in the mood to…you know."

The door suddenly swung open with Sam telling the dogs to be quiet. He looked flushed and his hair was ruffled. "Hi, Denise, hi, Redford. Welcome to our home." He laughed. "Our noisy home."

I said hello and the men shook hands. Tingling with embarrassment, I stepped inside the beautifully decorated log cabin. From the looks of Sam, we had definitely arrived in the middle of…something.

Kenzie appeared from a hall, barefoot and running. "Denise! It's so good to see you!"

We hugged. "You, too…new mama. Er, I tried to call, but my battery died."

"Oh, that's okay, we were just…cleaning. So that's Redford?" she whispered in my ear. "Yowsa. He looks like that and he has a big—"

"Kenzie—" I cut in, my voice a warning. "I'm an engaged woman."

"Don't worry," she said out of the corner of her mouth. "I won't say anything…suggestive. And Sam and I will be on our best behavior all afternoon."

"Good," I said. "By the way…your blouse is on backward."

"Great news, Kenzie," Sam said from the doorway. "Redford has a double-cab pickup—there's room for you and Denise to ride along."

Kenzie clapped her hands, then looked at me. "Oh, Denise, is that okay? I thought we'd stay here, but there's a pony at Valla Farms that Sam and I want to look at."

I stared at her. Kenzie Mansfield used to be the most cosmopolitan woman I knew and now she stood barefoot and pregnant in a log cabin, talking about ponies? What had happened to the woman I knew?

She'd fallen in love with a man and lost herself.

"I don't like horses," I murmured.

"Are you up for it?" Redford asked, his eyebrows raised in question. He held his hat in his hands and— Good grief, he was so...appealing.

"Come on," Kenzie urged in my ear. "It'll be fun." Then she winked. "Besides, horses can be kind of sexy."

Great. Just...great.

15

"RELAX," REDFORD URGED.

Easier said than done, considering I was astride a mammoth creature capable of tossing me off like a rag doll and trampling me beneath its razor-sharp hooves. Worse, Redford sat behind me on the beast, thigh to thigh, his arms loosely around mine, demonstrating the proper position for holding the reins.

I could barely breathe, but I murmured, "I'm relaxed," over my shoulder.

"Your back is a ramrod, and your arms are like rebar."

"I don't know what that is."

"Trust me, it's stiff."

His sexy voice rumbling in my ear wasn't helping matters. Plus I felt like an idiot wannabe, wearing my riveted jeans, embroidered shirt, horse sweater, and suede fringe jacket. Kenzie had loaned me a pair of her Doc Martens—they were snug, but had weathered the random piles of horse poo that littered the stable floor. However, there was no piece of equipment that could stem the pungent odor of horseflesh…ugh—it was an acquired smell, at best.

But the owners of Valla Farms had been accommodating…while they prepared the stud that Redford was interested in, he had asked to saddle one of their trail horses to help me, he said, to get over my fear of horses. I had been reluctant (a slight understatement), until I started feeling like a sissy as Kenzie and Sam had pleaded with me to give it a try. I had acquiesced, frankly, to get it over with.

Now, as I was being jolted around on the saddle atop "Reggie," I was regretting my weakness. Sissies got the last laugh—they lived longer.

"The horse can sense your fear," Redford said into my ear. "Loosen up—try to get in synch with the animal, to anticipate its movement. It's not unlike making love."

I jerked my head around. "You're not helping."

He chuckled in my ear. "Okay, I'll be quiet."

As we walked in a circle, I tried to do what Redford said, to loosen my muscles and my joints, to sway with the horse, not against it.

"That's good," he murmured.

"I feel like I could fall off."

"Use your thighs and knees to hang on."

His unspoken words "not unlike making love" hung in the air.

"Besides, I'm not going to let you fall."

But when I pressed my knees into Reggie, he startled and picked up speed.

"What did I do?" I cried.

"Maintain even pressure with your knees—when you squeeze, he thinks you want him to speed up."

Not unlike making love. With Redford's chest pressed up against my back and being cocooned in his arms, my imagination—and memory—didn't have far to leap to make the connection.

"By the way, I like your sweater," he said. "Looks familiar."

I decided not to answer. Explaining that I'd been on the verge of giving it away seemed too complicated. But knowing that he remembered the sweater put a warm feeling in my stomach…and lower.

I forced myself to concentrate on the efficiency of the horse's movements, and Redford's. Soon I was rocking rhythmically in the saddle, pleased to be getting the hang of it…until I became aware of something else entirely. Where the saddle rose up in front of me, it was applying pressure to my womanly regions… And the more relaxed I became, the more the pressure hit…*home.* Panicked, I glanced from side to side. Was this normal?

"That's it," Redford murmured in my ear. "Now you're getting the hang of it."

Indeed. It was like dancing—my shoulders flowing, my hips rocking. I was at the perfect angle to be stroked by the hard leather saddle with every stride, and I could feel myself growing warm and moist. Being sandwiched between Redford's muscular body and the powerful horse was one of the most erotic things I'd ever experienced. With a start, I realized that if I didn't stop, the inevitable would happen. And if I had an orgasm right here and now, I'd have to throw myself under the horse to be trampled because I'd never be able to face Redford or my friends—or anyone—again.

"I'm ready to stop," I said suddenly.

Something in my voice must have convinced him not to argue because he said, "Okay. Gently pull back on the reins, and say, 'whoa.'"

I did, and to my amazement, the horse stopped.

"See, not so hard," Redford said, sliding down first. Then he talked me through dismounting properly, and quickly, so the horse wouldn't move. When my second foot landed—in squishy poo—I felt a little unsteady, not to mention light-headed, from using dormant muscles and from my secret little sensual experience. Redford steadied me with his hand and gave me a wink. "You're a natural."

Despite the cold, my cheeks felt warm from his praise. I was exhilarated, flush with accomplishment…and heightened physical awareness. "Liar. But thank you, Redford. It was…fun."

"Good," he said, his dark eyes sincere. "I'm glad I could introduce you to a new experience."

I realized that every time I was with Redford, he introduced me to new things—things I wouldn't have done on my own—and wound up liking. I couldn't look away from his gaze, and felt a new, sizzling connection with him. My sensitized areas tingled and I was at a loss for words.

A man entered the stable yard and told Redford they were ready in the broodmare barn. (From my reading, I knew that was a place where the girl horses stayed until they were ready to…you know.) Redford handed off the horse we'd been riding to the man and the four of us walked to the long, narrow building the man indicated.

There the scent of horseflesh was overpowering. The barn was lined on both sides with unbelievably nice stables, each door adorned with a brass plate with the occupant's name on it. The horses themselves weren't visible, but we could hear them moving around and occasionally neighing.

A man who identified himself as the foreman shook our hands and welcomed us to Valla Farms. "Mr. DeMoss, I understand you're here to find a teaser stud to take back to Kentucky."

"That's right," Redford said with a nod.

"We have a horse I think you're going to like. His name is Henry—he's part draft horse."

"Sounds good," Redford said. "I'd like to see him in action."

"I'll bring him in now, sir."

The foreman moved away from us and I asked Redford, "The stud isn't a Thoroughbred?"

"No. I'm looking for a teaser stud, not a stallion. Thoroughbreds don't make good teasers—they're too high-strung."

I frowned. "What's a 'teaser' stud?"

He nodded toward the big gray horse being led in. "You'll see."

"Henry" was neighing—squealing really, lifting his big head as if he were calling out to the horses in the stalls. The foreman checked a clipboard, then pointed to the first stall. The man leading Henry opened the stall door, then stood back as Henry stuck his head in.

Blam! I jumped as the mare delivered a swift kick with her rear hoof that zoomed past Henry's head and landed against the stall door. Henry seemed to take the reaction in stride as he backed away and waited patiently as the handler closed the door, moved down two stalls and opened another one. Again Henry stuck his head in, sniffing the air, emitting a low squeal. The mare inside, after a bit of stamping and shuffling, lifted her tail and urinated. A bit gross from my perspective, but Henry seemed satisfied and retreated. The foreman made notes on his clipboard and directed the handler where to take him next.

Henry made his way down the stable row, sticking his head in and dodging powerful kicks when necessary, or neighing and rearing his head when a mare backed up to him and flipped her tail.

I wasn't an expert, but I took a wild guess that tail-flipping was a signal that she wouldn't mind being mounted. Except instead of obliging, Henry would whinny and back out, moving on to the next mare.

"A teaser stud," Redford said in my ear, "gets the

mare excited so when the high-strung and high-dollar Thoroughbred stallion struts in, she'll be ready."

The analogy wasn't lost on me. A hot flush bloomed on my chest and scalded my neck. Since Redford's arrival Friday, I'd been in a near-constant state of arousal. He was intimating that he was getting me worked up, and Barry would get the benefit. Knowing that Redford knew he was getting to me only made me more uncomfortable…and more aroused. I couldn't look at him, didn't trust my reaction. But I realized with dismay that the sex life of animals and the sex life of humans was more alike than different—both were complicated.

By the end of the exercise, Henry was…stirred up, giving me my first look at a stallion's penis. (I could strike that item from my life list.) I was duly impressed…and a little fearful for the mares. Henry must have known he wasn't getting any action today, though, because he lost his erection as soon as the last stable door closed. Redford asked the foreman more questions about the stud while he patted down the horse. Sam also looked the horse over, checking teeth, eyes and hooves, and removing a stethoscope to listen to the horse's organs.

It was hard for me to take my eyes off Redford, though. Seeing him in his natural environment was mesmerizing. He was a big man, could hold his own against a behemoth like Henry when he started to prance around. While still talking, Redford grabbed the lead rope and settled the horse down within seconds.

"He's something," Kenzie whispered.

I turned to look at her. "The horse?"

"No, not the horse, silly—Redford."

"Um…yes, Redford knows his way around horses."

Kenzie angled her head. "He seems to know his way around you, too. Are you sure there's no unfinished business between the two of you?"

I looked at her, my throat and chest tight. "I'm engaged, Kenzie."

She narrowed her eyes. "But you're not married yet. If you still have feelings for this man, Denise, you'd better find closure now rather than later, when so many lives will be upended."

Her dialogue was cut short by the appearance of Sam. "Kenzie, are you ready to look at that pony?"

"Oh, yes! Let's go."

Redford was shaking hands with the foreman when we walked up, making plans to talk again after he returned to Kentucky. I felt a sad little pang thinking about him leaving, but reminded myself that I, too, would soon be swept back into my regular life.

The four of us followed the handler to a barn, where he handed off Henry, then were led to another building that he called the birthing barn. Inside were more stalls, equally as fancy as in the broodmare barn. He led us to one on the end and opened the stall door. Inside, a brown mother and her leggy gray foal stood nuzzling.

Kenzie fell in love instantly. "Oh, isn't it the most precious thing you've ever seen?"

Sam agreed, but seemed more interested in checking out the foal's physique.

"This here is Henry's foal," the handler said.

I looked at Redford. "So he does get to…um…"

Redford laughed, his eyes merry, then he leaned down. "Eventually you have to let the teaser stud go all the way, or he loses interest altogether."

My skin burned. Was his remark a veiled threat… or a promise? Was Redford implying that this was my last chance? His expression looked innocent enough, but I knew Redford well enough to know that there wasn't anything innocent about him.

Kenzie and Sam arranged to come back to get the foal, and Kenzie chattered about it nonstop as we started back to their house. How she wanted their baby to grow up around horses and to have his or her own pony. Sitting in the back seat with her, I nodded, pretending to listen. But I was actually still pondering her earlier warning—if I had unresolved feelings for Redford, I should explore them now, while Redford was here and before I married Barry.

Throughout the day, the skies had grown increasingly leaden, the temperature increasingly colder. And within a few minutes of getting on the road, we encountered freezing rain.

"I was afraid this was going to happen," Redford said, shifting into a lower gear.

"Don't worry—we have plenty of room for the two of you to spend the night," Kenzie piped up.

The panic must have been apparent on my face because she quickly added, "The apartment over the clinic has two beds."

Which made the atmosphere in the cab of the truck less awkward, for sure.

She gave me an apologetic smile. "I guess I cleared out the guest room in the cabin a bit prematurely."

My pulse began to race—not at the imminent danger of the weather, but at the possibility of being holed up with Redford. Even if we weren't in the same bed, it smacked of familiarity, of intimacy.

And if we *were* in the same bed—

I massaged my temples and puffed out my cheeks in a long exhale—under no circumstances would we be in the same bed.

Then, somewhere from the depths of my brain, in a dark corner that remembered the time in Vegas, an idea formed and an inner voice gave it life: *This is your chance...spend the night with Redford...get it out of your system...it can't be as good as you remember...then you'll know that Redford isn't the fantasy man you've built him up to be in your mind...you can marry Barry with a clear heart, if not a clear conscience...*

The thought circled in my head until I was sure I had ruts worn into my brain. Suddenly I realized that everyone was looking at me, and for one mortifying moment, I thought I'd spoken aloud. Then I realized that we were back at Kenzie and Sam's. Good grief, how long had I been zoned out?

Kenzie touched my arm. "Redford said it was up to you. Can you take a day of vacation tomorrow and spend the night here?"

Darkness had fallen quickly and ice coated the truck windows, except for the windshield. Freezing rain pinged on the glass. My watch read 6:30 p.m. It would be a treacherous drive back to Manhattan. But from Redford's solemn expression in the rearview mirror, I knew if I wanted to go, he would deliver me home safely, even if it took all night to get there.

Preserving my chastity, however, didn't seem worth risking both our lives for. Not simply to make a point. And not simply to remove temptation from my path.

I wet my lips. "I can take a day of vacation tomorrow." Although, ironically, it might mean one less day I could take for my honeymoon.

"Whew, that's a relief," Kenzie said.

I caught Redford's gaze in the mirror, and there was something burning in his eyes, but I can't say it was relief. Hope? I pressed my lips together, wondering if I'd made a decision that I'd regret in the morning…if not before.

"Brrr, let's get inside and warm up," Kenzie said, then grinned. "And I think the men should fix chili for dinner."

Sam frowned over the front seat. "I thought spicy foods made you nauseous."

"Not today," she sang. "I'm craving peppers."

Sam looked at Redford. "Looks like we have kitchen duty."

Redford nodded. "Fair enough."

"Everyone head for the back door," Kenzie said. "We can shed wet clothes in the mudroom."

We sprinted through the icy rain, me slipping and sliding my way toward the house. Redford grabbed my hand and kept me upright. We were both laughing by the time we reached the back door. When we bounded into the mudroom, I didn't want to let go. Redford gave my hand a final squeeze, then we peeled off our wet jackets and boots in silence as Kenzie chattered on about the weather.

Dinner was fun, like a commercial about friends. Kenzie put on some music. The guys donned aprons and made chili and drank beer while Kenzie and I sat at the breakfast bar with our own drinks—beer for me, soda for her—and teased them. Redford seemed comfortable helping out in the kitchen. He and Sam even bantered about what secret ingredient made the best chili. I don't know why it surprised me that Redford could look sexy in a chef's apron, but it did. I sat at the bar and watched him move and interact with my friends as if he'd known them all of his life.

Sam and Kenzie asked him about the Corps, about Kentucky and about his family stables. I hung on every word. It was my chance to know the answers to all the questions I'd wanted to ask since he'd arrived, but had been afraid of delving into too deeply.

Redford talked about his career as a Marine with pride and fondness for the men and women he'd served with. But he said he was happy to be retired from the military at an age when he could still pursue another career. When he talked about Kentucky and his family stables, his voice took on an unmistakable warmth. It was clear he loved the place, and the horse business.

And it was clear to me that the woman in his life would have to do the same.

"So you're going back as soon as the IRS audit is over?" Kenzie asked Redford.

He glanced at me before he answered her. "That's the plan."

"Well, you don't have to worry about the audit," Kenzie said. "Denise is a money genius. She saved me and Sam thousands this year on our taxes."

Redford looked back to me and grinned. "I could sure use a money genius to help me grow the stables, if you can give me a referral."

I squirmed on my bar stool. "I'll give you the name of someone local that my firm has worked with."

"That'd be great," he said easily, lifting his beer bottle, but maintaining eye contact while he drank.

"Soup's on," Sam announced. "Or rather… chili's on."

We moved to the table and Redford held out my chair. I sat slowly, ultra-aware of his closeness crowding me as he scooted me in. The food was good, but my appetite was nil as I watched the clock move toward bedtime. I felt the pressure of a decision encroaching—I suspected that Redford would not turn me away from his bed.

I slanted a glance in his direction under my lashes.

On the other hand, maybe he had tired of my uncertainty and had decided not to get in the middle of my life.

"Oh," Kenzie said suddenly, covering her mouth. "I don't...feel...so well. Excuse me."

She fled in the direction of the bathroom, and Sam went after her.

I winced at Redford and he looked sympathetic. "Must be rough."

"Yeah, she looked green."

"No, I mean on Sam."

I gave him a light punch in the shoulder, which he tried to dodge. Then I pushed to my feet to clear the table. He stood to help, gathering bottles and glasses.

"I'm sorry, Denise."

I looked up, surprised. "About what?"

"About convincing you to come with me today. Now we're stuck here and you have to miss work tomorrow.... I know you have better things to do."

I loaded the dishwasher with our bowls and utensils. "It was my decision to come, Redford." I turned to look at him, dead-on. "And it was my decision to stay."

He dropped a glass, but caught it before it hit the floor. Then he looked at me, his expression cautious.

"Denise, I can stay here and bunk down on the couch or floor." A smile curved his mouth. "With the dogs."

Chivalrous to a fault. It was crazy, but I wanted to be close to him tonight, even if nothing happened between us. I moistened my lips. "That seems silly when there are two beds in the apartment."

Desire flickered in his dark eyes before he glanced away. When he looked back, he seemed calm...or resolute. "Okay."

"Sorry, folks," Sam announced, walking back into the kitchen. "Looks like Kenzie is out for the night."

"Is she going to be okay?" I asked.

"Oh, sure. I knew she'd regret the chili, but you can't tell that woman anything. I'll walk you to the clinic and get you settled in."

He produced a stack of clothes. "These should help tide you over for tonight. There's a washer and dryer in the apartment, plus a television and a phone if you need to make calls. Lots of hot water for a shower." He caught himself. "Or two." Then he burst out whistling, presumably to keep from putting his foot in his mouth.

My skin felt prickly on the short walk to the clinic, and it wasn't the rain because it had stopped. Everything—every blade of grass, every twig—was coated with a layer of ice. The yard looked like a winter wonderland, glistening like diamonds beneath the dusk-to-dawn light. The ground crunched beneath our feet, but water dripped from the utility lines—a good sign that the temperature was rising above freezing and we'd be able to leave in the morning.

But frankly, I could barely think past tonight.

Sam unlocked the door of the clinic and led us

through a lobby, down a long hall past an office and an examination room, and up a flight of stairs.

"This is where I lived while I built the cabin," he explained, opening a door and flipping a light on inside.

And where Kenzie had stayed when she'd visited Sam to write the article, I recalled.

The suite was spacious, with a combination bedroom/living room/kitchen area containing two twin beds—that seemed to scream at me—an overstuffed couch and chair situated around a television, and an efficiency-size kitchen. A separate bathroom contained a washer/dryer closet and was stocked with toiletries.

Sam nodded to one long window facing the cabin. "It'll be warmer if you keep the curtains closed," he said, then he coughed into his hand and strode back to the doorway. "Call us if you need anything."

My feet itched with the sudden urge to run past him and back to the cabin. I could bunk down on one of their couches, if the dogs were willing to share. My knees were literally trembling. I was in a full sweat.

"Thank you, Sam," Redford said, then glanced in my direction, his eyebrow raised slightly. He was offering me an out. No doubt my nerves were palpable. I took in his face and the body that could turn me on with a twitch—and I panicked.

"Sam!" I cried.

Sam turned back. "Yeah, Denise?"

There are a few defining moments in every person's life, when one simple decision can change the person they are, and the person they become. I knew in my heart of hearts, this was one of those moments.

"Thanks," I said, managing a smile, "for your hospitality."

"No problem. See you two in the morning."

The door closed, and I felt rooted to the floor.

Redford removed his coat, hung his black hat on the post of one of the beds and jammed his big hands on his hips…waiting. Waiting for a sign, either way. Morning was hours and hours away. How would we spend those hours?

"Denise," he said finally, his voice low and hoarse. "I'm tired of beating around the bush here."

(It was, admittedly, a fitting sexual interpretation of the saying.) My heart thudded in my chest in anticipation of his next words.

"I want you in my bed tonight, but the choice is entirely yours."

Desire flooded my body, rushing through my veins, awakening every nerve ending. The silence stretched between us for long seconds, while my mind raced with uncertainty. "I…" I swallowed and tried again, not entirely sure what words might tumble out of my mouth. "I…excuse me."

I escaped to the bathroom, closed the door behind me and leaned against it with a long exhale. I was steamy from wearing my fringe suede coat, which was still damp. I shrugged out of my coat, but the weight wasn't lifted from my shoulders. I stared at myself in the mirror, touched my skin, my hair, concrete things that defined me, things I knew to be true because I saw them in the mirror every day. But what about the things I couldn't see? What about those deep, dark desires that lurked in my heart? Those things defined me, too, whether I liked it or not.

I didn't like it, knowing that my body could override my reason. But I moistened my lips with my tongue and acknowledged how much I wanted Redford, how much I wanted to share his bed tonight. Worse, I *needed* to do this.

With shaking hands, I slipped my engagement ring from my finger and set it on the vanity, then opened the door, inhaled deeply and walked out to the bedroom.

16

REDFORD'S BACK was to me when I emerged from the bathroom, and when he turned, I was afraid I would lose my nerve. But when I saw his handsome face, his powerfully built body, his questioning eyes, my hunger for him exploded, and I rushed into his arms.

He caught me up against him, practically lifting me off the ground as he kissed me deeply, crushing me in his embrace. Our meeting was feverish, our breathing ragged, our hands rushed as we tore at each other's clothes. His shirt fell away, then his T-shirt, my sweater, shirt and jeans. I smoothed my hands up the wide expanse of his chest, the dark crisp hairs tickling my palms. His was a working man's body—corded with muscle, lean and tan. I closed my eyes, reveling in the smooth skin of his back, the indention of his spine, the tapering of his waist. Dark hair converged on the flat planes of his stomach into a line that disappeared into the waist of his jeans that, without his belt, barely hung on his hips, revealing the elastic waistband of his white boxers.

Experiencing the textures of his body, combined with his exploration of mine, made me breathless. He cupped my breasts through my flimsy bra, teasing the budded nipples. I don't have a model body, but my breasts are my one asset. Did he remember how much I loved him touching them?

Yes, I decided when he unhooked my bra and dropped to his knees to kiss and lick each pink peak thoroughly, dragging his teeth across the sensitive skin, sending instant moisture to wet my thin panties. I cried out, my hands kneading his neck, my knees buckling. I fell forward and he picked me up, then carried me to one of the beds, settling me on the edge and rolling my panties down the length of my legs.

He spread my knees and knelt to rain kisses up my inner thighs, moving back and forth, nipping at my skin. I leaned back on my elbows because in addition to the unbelievable sparkles of pleasure of having his mouth on me, in addition to the almost unbearable anticipation of having his tongue *inside* me, I took great pleasure in watching Redford enjoy the act of making love to me with his mouth. When he reached the culmination of his journey, his warm tongue flicked against my wet folds and our moans melded. Seeing his dark head between my thighs was incredibly erotic.

When he plunged his tongue inside me, my body jerked in response to the icy fire racing through my muscles. After teasing me mercilessly, he found my sensual switch and worked it with his tongue until I clenched my fists in the bedspread, murmuring his name, begging for release. He moaned against my clit to escalate the vibrations, launching me to an orgasm so powerful, that even in the throes of the intense spasms, the possibility of a health implication crossed my mind—a burst vein, a permanent muscle contraction, a heart attack.

But happily, I lived to reach for his waistband and unzip his jeans, feeling another surge of desire when I freed his enormous erection. He groaned, then sucked in a sharp breath when I pushed down his soft cotton boxers to cradle his sex in my hands.

I had hinted—okay, *bragged*—to my friends at Redford's massive size. I had dreamed of his nude body countless times, had conjured up his image for dozens of erotic sessions alone and—I'm not proud to admit—when in bed with other men. But when I saw and felt his rigid, straining shaft, I was awed all over again…thick and long, with an enormous tip, already shiny with pre-come. I dipped my head for a taste, but Redford stopped me with a groan.

"Don't think I don't want you to," he gasped. "But I'm so hot for you right now, I won't last two seconds. And I want to be inside you…the first time."

A pang of longing struck me low and hard. I nodded my agreement, then almost panicked. "Do you have protection?"

He grinned sheepishly. "At the risk of seeming presumptuous, I came prepared."

At the moment, I didn't care about his motivation

for bringing condoms, I was just weak with relief that he'd brought them. He retrieved one from his wallet, then handed it to me. With him standing in front of me seated on the edge of the bed, I rolled it on carefully, conscious of his size and our safety. Then reached down to caress his velvety sack and the sensitive ridge beneath—things I'd never done to any other man. He clenched my shoulders in a long moan, then urged me back on the bed. He followed me, stretching out on top of me, bracing himself with his arms. The sensation of full-body contact with him almost overwhelmed me—and I knew there was so much more to come.

He kissed me hard, slanting his mouth over mine, delving his tongue deep, sharing my essence with me. He captured my hands, entwining our fingers, and pinned them to the bed over my head. Our bodies were slick with perspiration, and the musk of his maleness only fueled my desire. "Now, Redford...now."

He shifted his hips, easing his erection between my thighs. His jaw was clenched with restraint as he found my entrance and pushed in slowly, one breathtaking inch at a time, until he was fully sheathed in my body. It was an amazing feeling, to be so filled, for every centimeter of my slick channel to be stimulated at once. I squeezed his fingers between mine and contracted my inner muscles around him.

"Oh, Denise," he groaned. "Oh, God, that feels... soooo...good."

He flexed his hips, making tiny thrusts that prodded an untapped spot deep inside me. Almost immediately, the waves of a powerful orgasm began to build, radiating from my womb. I flailed as the tension in my body mounted. His thrusts intensified—longer, deeper, faster. Our moans mingled as the sensations ratcheted higher. I climaxed in a sudden explosion of color and light, and sank my teeth into his shoulder to stifle my cries. His shuddering release came a split second after mine, his face contorted in pleasure-pain, my name on his lips.

Our "little death" coincided exactly with the death of the twin bed. One lower corner fell to the floor, giving us a good bounce on the box springs, then the post fell over with a thud.

We collapsed into each other laughing, our skin flushed and hot to the touch and wet with exertion. "Looks like we'll be sleeping in the other bed," he muttered.

Then he rolled me over on top of him and exhaled noisily. "That," he murmured, "was amazing."

I sighed against his chest, feeling languid and blissful, my body still pulsing from the pleasure he'd given me. "I have a confession to make."

He tensed. "What?"

"I almost got off while I was riding that horse today."

Two seconds of dead silence was split open by his howl of laughter.

I swatted at his chest. "It's not that funny."

"Yes, it is," he said, whooping. "No wonder you wanted to get down from there so fast."

"It's your fault."

"How?"

"You goaded me into riding that beast."

He emitted a low growl. "If I'd known what was going on up there, I would've made old Reggie gallop."

"Gee, thanks for not making me feel like an idiot."

He laughed. "Don't be so hard on yourself. I've heard of it happening before."

"You have?"

"Well, only with extraordinarily horny women."

"Oh, you!" I pushed up to move away, but he captured my wrist.

"Where do you think you're going?"

"To take a shower."

"Not without me, you're not."

Warmth filtered through my chest as he pushed to his feet and pulled me into the bathroom. He closed the door and pinned me against the door. "But first, I have to do something that I've been dying to do since I got here."

Full of female pride, I grinned. "I thought we just did that."

He laughed. "Yes, but there's one more thing."

He reached behind my neck and gently, ever so gently, he released my hair from its clasp and pushed his hands into it, pulling it forward around my shoulders. "Beautiful," he breathed.

I couldn't speak. The feelings welling up in my

chest... I didn't even want to think about what they might mean.

He kissed me lightly. "You like the water hot, don't you?"

I nodded, inordinately pleased he remembered.

While he turned on the water and adjusted the temperature, I leaned against the vanity, enjoying the view of his lean backside and powerful hamstrings. And the treasure on the other side...*sigh.* Lust pumped through my body with such force that I pressed a fist to my mouth to regain control. This man brought out the worst in me.

Out of the corner of my eye, I caught sight of my engagement ring on the vanity where I'd left it. With much effort, I pushed down the spike of guilt, and when Redford turned around, I reached out and flipped off the light.

A few seconds later his chuckle reverberated in the tiled room. "It's a little late for shyness, don't you think, Denise?"

Seizing a deliciously wicked opportunity, I pushed off the vanity, felt my way over to him and pressed my breasts into his warm back. "I thought we could take a shower in the dark."

He gave a low laugh of compliance and we climbed under the spray together.

When one sense is taken away, the other senses truly do become more keen. With the door closed, the windowless room was completely dark, and suddenly, I could feel the smooth surface of the tub beneath my feet, the softness of the country water splashing over my face, the callused tips of Redford's hands caressing my bottom.

I wrapped my arms around his waist and flicked my tongue over his nipples, reveling in the saltiness of his skin. I felt around the wall until I found a soft loofah and what felt like a new bar of soap. I lathered the loofah and scrubbed Redford's back in large, massaging circles, applying as much pressure as I could.

"Ooh, that's great," he moaned.

The acoustics in our little cocoon were wonderful, magnifying our noises. Methodically, I worked the loofah over his shoulders and down his arms, then down to his lower back and hips. I turned him around slowly and massaged the lather onto his chest, ignoring for the time being his erection prodding my stomach. He submitted to my ministrations, murmuring approval as I moved across his stomach and hip bones, then moved down to his thighs. I knelt to better feel my way down the fronts of his legs, then handed him the loofah and the soap. Still kneeling, I gently washed his cock with my hands, massaging and stroking him clean. Then I took the velvety tip into my mouth, eliciting a gasp from Redford. The water spilled over my hair and face as I pleasured him with my mouth, taking in as much of his length as I could accommodate, stroking the base of him with my fingers.

With a guttural groan, Redford stopped me, lifted me to my feet and whispered, "Your turn." He moved behind me and began to massage my neck and shoulders. I sighed in appreciation, planting my hands against the shower wall, allowing the spray to wash over my face. While he moved the loofah over my back, he slid his hand around to massage my breasts. It was ecstasy, feeling so many sensations and textures at once—and knowing that with Redford, the best was yet to come.

He worked the loofah down my back and over my hips, while sliding his other hand down my stomach and into the curls between my thighs. "Mmm, ohhh, yesssss."

"You like?" he whispered.

"Umm-hmm."

He slipped a finger inside me from behind. "You like?" he whispered.

"Ummm-hmmm." I contracted around him, and he pressed forward. The man knew how to push my button, from both sides. I could feel another orgasm coming on and gave in to it, brought to higher heights with every stroke at his urging in my ear. When one wave subsided, another crashed through my body, vibrating me down to my bones. At last, when I was too weak to stand, Redford supported me with one hand and turned off the shower with the other.

Unfortunately, I slipped and threw him off balance, too. I could feel us going down and grabbed for the shower curtain, which came crashing down with us, but helped to break our fall.

"Are you okay?" he asked.

"Fine," I moaned. "You?"

"Yeah, I think so."

I started giggling. "So much for showering in the dark."

We both laughed until we were limp, then wrapped towels around ourselves and went back to the other room, where we rubbed each other down.

Of course, the rubbing led to other touching, and the touching lead to kissing, and the kissing led to us concluding that both the crippled bed and the other twin bed were simply too small.

"We can push them together," I suggested, and Redford agreed. But when they were about two feet apart, his eyes lit up.

"What?" I asked.

He moved to stand between the beds, then urged me up, to straddle the beds—to straddle him. I grinned, then looped my arms around his neck and whispered naughty things in his ear until his erection was so stiff, I could have impaled myself on him. Instead, I leveraged myself on the two beds and lowered myself on him bit by thrilling bit as he nuzzled my breasts.

The position was mind-blowing, matching up our boy and girl parts perfectly, allowing Redford to reach my highest secret places, and providing enough frontal friction that another orgasm for me was only a matter of time. Our hands were free to roam, and best of all: we could look into each other's eyes.

Redford had the sexiest eyes—endlessly deep and

expressive. I could tell every time he reached a new pleasure plateau. When my body began to tremble with the onset of a powerful climax, he curled his hand around the nape of my neck and brought my face up to his.

"I want to see you come," he said. "I want to see your face, see how I make you feel."

His words sent me soaring over the edge, my already sensitized erogenous zones screaming with release. I clung to him while spasms racked my body. He uttered a long, quaking groan and picked me up, climaxing with my arms and legs wrapped around him like a vise. It was a religious experience.

When our bodies quieted, we found that we had somehow traveled several feet away from the bed. He looked for a place to lower me, and we almost made it to the couch. My dismount was wobbly and I hooked a floor lamp on my way down, sending it crashing to the floor, crushing the shade and shattering the bulb.

We were trashing Kenzie and Sam's place...but I knew if anyone would understand, they would.

We decided to sleep where we fell, on the couch. My body was fatigued beyond words, but my mind wouldn't shut down so easily. I lay with my head on Redford's chest and listened as his heart quieted, then fell into a steady sleep rhythm. Slowly, like a leaky dyke, my troubles seeped through the sex-haze I had immersed myself in for the past couple of hours, until I was saturated in shame.

What had I done? Had sex with a man I had no intention of having a relationship with—and every indication that he felt the same. Hadn't he thanked me for filing the annulment papers? For the second time, we had been brought together on a whim, enjoyed each other's bodies and would separate.

Except he would go back to the life he'd planned for himself without breaking stride, while the life that I'd planned for myself—with Barry—had been compromised. What was I thinking? I had a *ring*. And I had a wedding dress, assuming Cindy managed to outbid SYLVIESMOM. Barry was in L.A., slaving away to build his career, to make a better life for both of us, and I was…here.

Naked with the man I'd married, then annulled myself from. Naked with my biggest mistake. Again.

A shiver passed over my body, the chill in the room seeking out the moist, naughty parts of me that still sang from Redford's touch. Unable to lie still any longer, I eased off the couch to make my way toward the bathroom. A few steps later, something sliced into the bottom of my foot, sending fire shooting up my leg. I cried out, and Redford was awake and on his feet before I could take another step.

"What happened?" he said, alarm in his voice.

I limped toward the bathroom. "I stepped on glass from the lightbulb…be careful."

He skirted the broken glass and followed me. "Let me take a look at it."

"No, that's okay," I said, fighting back tears…as

much for the pain radiating in my foot as for the situation I'd landed myself in. "Just clean up the glass."

In the bathroom, I swept aside the torn shower curtain and broken rod and lowered myself to the edge of the tub. The amount of blood staining the white tile floor was distressing, but when I stuck my foot under cold running water, I was relieved to discover it was actually a small wound. Still, my eyes overflowed and I was shaking. My engagement ring glittered from the vanity. I reached over and picked it up, then slid it onto my finger, my tears coming in earnest now.

"Are you okay?" Redford said from the doorway.

I looked up, then hastily brushed at my cheeks and nodded. "It's not as bad as it looks." I pulled the shower curtain over me—it was much too late for modestly, but still.

"Let me take a look," he said gently. "To make sure the glass is out."

I yielded, lifting my foot and swiveling. He cradled my foot in his big hand, then pinched open the cut. I flinched.

"Sorry," he said, then patted my foot. "But it looks clean. Let me see if I can find a bandage. I'm sure Sam has plenty of supplies around." He rummaged in the vanity, then removed a bottle of peroxide and a box of adhesive bandages.

I was still while he dressed the wound, my throat and chest tight. He occasionally glanced to my left hand, at the ring, but he didn't say anything.

"Does it hurt?" he asked finally.

I wiped at more tears, but shook my head. I couldn't tell him why I was crying. I wasn't even sure myself.

He made a rueful noise. "It will in the morning."

I swallowed in resignation.

I was pretty sure that everything would be hurting in the morning.

17

KENZIE OPENED the back door when I knocked the next morning. "Good morning."

"Good morning," I said with as much nonchalance as I could muster considering every muscle in my body screamed with pain.

Her smile was questioning, but she simply sipped from her coffee cup while I followed her into the kitchen.

"You're limping," she said, pointing.

I stacked the unused clothes that Sam had loaned us on the table and lowered myself onto a bar stool. "Um, we had a little accident last night."

"We?" she asked.

I squirmed. "I hope the furnishings in the apartment weren't family heirlooms."

Her eyes widened. "Did you set a fire, too?"

"No, thank God. But one of the beds is broken, the shower curtain is torn and the curtain rod snapped… and the floor lamp is history. Oh, and there are a few, um, bloodstains on the carpet."

She frowned. "What?" Then she gave a dismissive wave. "Don't worry about the furniture, it's all secondhand. But what on earth did you two do over there?"

My face flamed. "I'd rather not talk about it."

She handed me a mug of coffee and smirked. "Is he as big as you remember?"

I took a deep drink. "Yes."

She gasped, her eyes dancing, until she spotted my engagement ring. "You're still wearing your ring?"

I shifted on the stool. "I took it off...*during*. Now things are...back to normal."

She looked worried. "So that's it, then. This thing with Redford was just a fling?"

"Right. It was always just sex between me and Redford. This was...my last hurrah before settling down."

"So he goes back to Kentucky—"

"And I stay in New York, where I belong," I finished.

Footsteps sounded in the mudroom, ending our conversation. Redford stuck his head in the kitchen. "Sorry, I knocked."

I busied myself drinking from my cup. Mine and Redford's conversation this morning had been brief and stilted. Worse, I could barely look at him without wanting to go at it again. I was pathetic.

"We don't stand on ceremony here, Redford," Kenzie said. "Come on in. Coffee?"

He wore his hat and coat, and his cheeks were red from the cold. "Sounds good." He glanced at me, his expression unreadable. "I started the truck to warm it up. Looks like the roads will be fine for the drive back."

"Good." I had called my office from the clinic and told them I wouldn't be in today.

Kenzie handed Redford a cup of coffee and he thanked her. "Sam's truck is gone. Has he left for the day?"

Kenzie nodded. "He asked me to give you his regrets. He got a call about an expectant cow mom in distress on a farm across the county." She grinned. "I figure if I get as big as a cow with this baby, he'll feel right at home."

"Are you feeling better this morning?" I asked, standing.

"Much."

"Are you coming back to the city this week?"

She sighed. "I hope so. I have to admit, I'm getting cabin fever on this mountain, especially since it's too cold to go outside. I miss the city. And you girls."

I gave her a hug. "Call me when you get back and we'll have lunch."

"You bet," she said. "Redford, it was a pleasure meeting you."

He nodded and thanked her for the hospitality. "Good luck with the baby." He smiled. "And with the foal."

She followed us to the door. "Good luck to you guys tomorrow on the audit."

I closed my eyes briefly—one more thing to dread.

The drive back to the city was, shall I say, *loooooong.* If we exchanged ten words, it was a lot. We listened to music and I plowed through the rest of the tax documents. But even though we didn't talk, Redford's body communicated with mine, sending out vibes that kept my senses on edge. Scenes from the previous night kept flashing into my mind. By the time we began to see signs for the city limits, I was almost frantic to be away from him.

"I left some cash in the apartment to cover the damages," he said suddenly.

"Oh…that was good of you."

"How's your foot?"

It throbbed. "It's okay, just a little sore."

He rolled his shoulders. "I'm sore all over."

I averted my gaze to my hands…and my ring.

He made a rueful noise in his throat. "I have the distinct feeling that you have regrets about last night."

I exhaled slowly and looked out the window. "Don't we all have regrets about things in our lives?"

"Absolutely. Vegas, for instance."

My chest tightened. "Right. Vegas." At least we agreed on one thing.

I was never so happy to see my apartment building. Redford pulled in to a rare empty parking space in front, then reached across the seat and picked up my hand. The gesture was unexpected, and sent my pulse spiking.

He rubbed his fingers across my palm. "Denise, I'm sorry about last night." He glanced up with a wry smile. "I feel like I'm always saying I'm sorry."

I swallowed hard. "Redford, you don't have to

apologize. You gave me a choice, and I made my decision. I went to you with my eyes wide open." I just hadn't realized my heart had been ajar, too.

He looked thoughtful and kept stroking my palm, sending little shivers up my arm. "It wasn't fair of me to put you in that position." He turned my hand over and fingered my engagement ring. "I know you feel guilty about what we did. I feel as if I've stormed through your life…again…and messed up your plans."

I didn't say anything, especially since I could barely speak when he touched me like that. He was trying to apologize for last night, and heaven help me, all I could think about was him kissing me again.

And suddenly, he *was* kissing me. First tenderly, then hungrily. We devoured each other, our tongues parlaying, our lips sliding, our teeth clicking. He hauled me across the seat into his lap and I ran my hands over his chest, his arms, drove my fingers into his hair.

"We could do it right here," he murmured raggedly, unbuttoning the top button of my blouse.

A memory chord vibrated…the very words I'd said to Barry, tempting him to do something naughty…

But when Redford stroked my nipple, I was willing to do anything he asked.

I loved him, I realized with a burst of adrenaline. *I loved this man.*

I returned his kiss like a starved woman, our hands roving, hunting for buttons, snaps.

A sharp rap on the window startled me—and Redford. My first thought was that it was the police and we were about to be booked for public indecency. But when I saw the astonished face of the person on the sidewalk, my stomach bottomed out.

"Mom?" I whispered.

"Mom?" Redford said, his voice panicked. "That woman is your mother?"

"And that man is my father," I murmured, utterly and completely horrified to see them staring in at us. Although, in fairness, they looked equally horrified. I slid off Redford's lap, straightening my clothes, gasping for air. "Omigod, omigod, omigod. Redford, when I get out, just drive away."

He frowned. "I'm not going to drive away like some teenage kid. I'm going to introduce myself to your father."

I was starting to hyperventilate. "I don't think that's a good idea."

"We've done a lot of things this weekend that weren't particularly bright. Come on."

There was no time to calm myself. I opened the truck door and climbed down, my heart jumping in my chest at the sight of my parents standing there, the epitome of upper-middle-classdom in their prim winter resort wear, surrounded by suitcases, looking shell-shocked.

"Mom…Dad…what a surprise."

My mother drew herself up. "That's obvious, dear."

"We tried to call you," my dad piped up, "but you

weren't answering your cell phone, or your phone at work. We thought we'd take our chances and see if you were home."

"I th-thought you were in *England*."

"The weather was miserable, so we decided to cut our trip short and stop here on our way home to congratulate you—" her eyes cut to Redford suspiciously "—on your engagement."

I wanted to evaporate. After a few seconds of gluey silence, I cleared my throat. "Um, Gayle and Harrison Cooke, this is Redford DeMoss."

Redford removed his hat and shook their hands. "How do you do, ma'am, sir?"

"And how do you know our Denise?" my mother asked sharply.

Oh...my...God.

Redford turned to me, his mouth slack with surprise. "Ma'am, I'll let Denise explain it." Then he put his hat back on his head. "After I leave you folks to enjoy your reunion."

Without being asked, he picked up the suitcases and carried them to the landing, then came back and tipped his hat. "Ma'am...sir...Denise." He looked at me, his eyes hard. "I'll see you tomorrow morning?"

The audit...of course. "I...I'll meet you there."

He nodded curtly, then climbed into his truck and drove away. My heart caved in when I saw him glance in the rearview mirror, then look away. Watching him leave was jarring to my senses. But I would have to get used to it.

I turned and gave my folks the best smile I could manage under the circumstances. "We need to talk."

My mother gave me a disapproving look. "I believe so."

I couldn't even bring myself to look at my poor dad—no doubt to his great relief. As we entered my apartment, I experienced age regression. By the time we had deposited their suitcases in a corner of the living room, I felt about twelve years old. The day of reckoning had arrived—the day my parents discovered that little Denise, squeaky-clean honor student who never caused them a day of trouble, wasn't perfect after all. Not even close. I thought I might be sick.

We had barely removed our coats before my mother crossed her arms and demanded, "Denise, *who* was that man you were *kissing* on the street?"

I turned to look at them and sighed. "Please sit down."

They sat on my couch and looked at me expectantly.

I took a deep breath and on the exhale said, "Redford and I were…married."

My mother clutched her chest. *"What? When?"*

"Three years ago."

She shrieked and grabbed my father's arm. "You're *married,* and you didn't even tell us?"

"No," I said, holding up my hand. "We *were* married. For six weeks. I had the marriage annulled."

My father looked completely lost. "Is that legal?"

"Yes. It means our marriage never happened."

He lifted his hands. "Who is this man and how did you meet him?"

Another deep breath. "I was in Vegas for the holidays. He was a Marine, on leave from the Gulf. That's where we met and…were married."

"In *Vegas?*" My mother looked horrified. "Harrison, it's our fault. That's the year we went on the Bahamas golf trip with the Sutherlands. If we'd stayed home, Denise would have been with us and this would never have happened." She teared up. "I didn't want to go on that trip—it was your idea—and just look what happened!"

Dad handed her his handkerchief. I pinched the bridge of my nose.

"Oh, Denise," she cried, "tell me the wedding at least took place in a church, not in one of those tacky chapels."

I winced. "It was in a tacky chapel." I cleared my throat—in for a penny, in for a pound. "Actually, in the drive-through."

My mother looked faint. "Harrison, get my heart pills."

My dad dutifully reached for Mom's purse and rummaged through the various prescriptions before handing her a bottle.

"Did that man take advantage of you?" he demanded. His face turned red. "Were you…with child?"

This was going well.

"No, Dad, no. Redford was…is a complete gentleman." I thought of the scene they'd witnessed outside and swallowed hard. "Ninety-nine percent of the time. We got married on the spur of the moment and when I came back to New York and he went back to the Gulf, we realized we'd made a mistake. That's all."

"That's all?" my mother asked. "Denise, marriage isn't something to take lightly."

I balked. "I know that. I'm not proud of what I did, which is why I didn't tell you."

"I don't understand," my dad said. "If you had the marriage annulled, then what is that man doing here?"

"He had to come to New York because our joint tax return is being audited by the IRS. We have an interview in the morning."

Now my dad looked truly horrified. "The IRS can ruin your life."

My mother's head bobbed. "Do you remember the McGoverns? Their 1040 form went astray and they lost their house. The IRS came and threw all their things out in the yard for anyone to take. Miriam lost her mother's silver—she said the mailman took it."

I rolled my eyes. "Mom, the IRS doesn't take that kind of action simply because a 1040 form wasn't filed. Besides, ours is just a routine audit." I hoped.

"Where does this young man live?" my dad wanted to know.

"Kentucky. He's retired from the Marines and works in his family stables."

My mother frowned. "He's a stable boy?"

"Um, no. They run a horse breeding business."

She made a face. (My utterance of the word "breeding" was as close to a "sex talk" as my mother and I had ever gotten.)

"So when did you and Barry break up?" she asked.

I swallowed. "We didn't."

Her gaze flew to my finger and she gasped, temporarily diverted. "Your ring is gorgeous!" She reached for my hand and scrutinized the diamond. "Oh, my, it looks flawless."

"It is."

She glanced up, then her eyes narrowed. "Where is Barry?"

"In L.A."

"So you're kissing this Redmon fellow in the street while your fiancé is out of town?"

"His name is Redford." And I was guilty of so much more than kissing.

"Your father and I raised you better than that, Denise."

I squirmed. "I'm sorry you and Dad had to see that. It…just happened…and it was a mistake."

She frowned. "Well, considering that ring on your finger, I hope it doesn't happen again. Why aren't you at work today?"

I didn't have time to think of a lie. "I went with Redford to upstate New York yesterday to look at a stud horse, and the weather was too bad for us to return last night."

My mother's eyebrows shot up and I didn't want

to know what was going through her mind. A lump formed in my throat and I felt very, very dirty.

My dad stood abruptly. "Gayle, we'd better go. Denise has a lot on her mind right now. Honey, we'll call you in a few days."

He gathered their coats and suitcases and shepherded my mother toward the door. But at the last minute, she turned back and wagged her finger at me. "Denise, a wise person learns from their mistakes."

KENZIE GASPED. "No, they didn't."

"Yes," I said into the phone miserably. "They did."

"Oh, my God, you were making out in his truck? In broad daylight?"

I closed my eyes. "Yes, but we weren't naked… yet." Thank goodness for small miracles.

"Well, what did you tell your parents?"

I sighed. "The truth."

"What did they say?"

I teared up. "They were shocked. My mother said that they raised me better than that, and then they left." I sniffed. "I can't imagine what they think of me."

Kenzie made a sympathetic noise. "They probably think that you're human, and that everyone makes mistakes. Give them some time to come around. Besides, Denise, you're an adult."

I pressed my lips together. "Which means I can be deceitful or even immoral without being accountable?"

"Of course not. But you have to decide for yourself what's right and what's wrong for *you*. You're the one who has to live with your mistakes."

"But my mistakes affect other people's lives, too."

"So explain to your mom that this thing between you and Redford was just a blip. That you were having cold feet after Barry proposed."

My throat ached from the lump that formed there. "Except I'm starting to think that it wasn't a blip... for me."

She gasped. "Are you in love with him again?"

"Maybe...yes."

"And what are you going to do about it?"

"Nothing. Kenzie, Redford *thanked* me for filing for the annulment, said it had allowed us to get on with our lives."

"So what about last night?"

I gave a little laugh. "Obviously, we're still attracted to each other. But sex is the only thing Redford and I have in common."

"It's about the only thing that Sam and I had in common."

"And look—" I stopped and bit my tongue.

"And look, what?" Kenzie asked lightly. "Look at how my life has changed?"

"Yes," I said finally.

"Hmm, let's see—before I met Sam I worked eighty hours a week and had no social life. Now I get to do the job I enjoy at a sane pace, and I have a husband who loves me and his baby in my belly." She sighed. "Denise, yes, my life has changed, and I couldn't be happier. I'm not saying that the way I did it would work for everyone, but sometimes you have to be willing to take a risk…like you did in Vegas."

I frowned. "But that was a disaster."

"Only because you came back and allowed everyone to convince you that it was a crazy thing to do."

"But it *was* a crazy thing to do."

"So? Just because it was crazy, doesn't mean it was a mistake."

I was quiet, digesting her words. "I guess I need more order in my life than most people. As much as I care about Redford, I just feel so…*reckless* when I'm around him. I can't live like that, Kenzie."

She sighed. "Then it sounds as if you've made the right decision to write this off as a fling and go on with your life."

I murmured my agreement, but I didn't feel as good as I'd hoped to feel.

"So, where is Redford tonight?"

"At his hotel, I assume. The scene with my parents caught him off guard, but he handled it well. Shook my father's hand and looked him in the eye before he left."

"Hmm…not easy to do after you've been caught with your pants down."

I sniffed. *"Tell me."*

"So he left?"

"He said he wanted to give us privacy. Basically, he was giving me an out if I wanted to lie to my parents. Again."

"Very chivalrous of him."

"Yes." Redford was nothing if not noble, which is why he would have stayed in a quickie Vegas marriage, even after he had realized his mistake. "Anyway, I'll see him tomorrow at the audit, and that will be the end of it."

Kenzie made a doubtful noise. "If you say so. Let me know how the audit goes."

I hung up the phone, leaden with despair. I found the plane tickets to Vegas I had bought as a Valentine's Day surprise for Barry and wavered. Maybe Barry and I simply didn't have enough fun together. Maybe I wasn't being fair. Then I stared at my laboratory-engineered-diamond engagement ring until my vision blurred. On top of everything else, the money already spent on our relationship was giving me an ulcer. And second thoughts.

With my heart pounding in my ears, I picked up the handset and dialed Barry's cell phone.

18

A SMALL PART OF ME hoped this was one of those times that Barry wouldn't answer his phone.

"Hello?" he answered on the first ring.

Apparently, I was not to be let off the hook so easily. I pressed my lips together to fight back tears.

"Hello?" he repeated, sounding tired.

"Hi," I croaked. "It's me...Denise."

"Oh, hi. I left you a couple of messages today at work."

"Um...I wound up taking the day off."

"Are you ill?"

Mentally, yes. "I'm fine, just needed to catch up on some things."

"I talked to Ellen this morning. She said she ran into you Saturday night at a Broadway show, that you were with some gay guy?"

I closed my eyes. "Um, yes...he's a...friend of mine."

"And she said the two of you are getting together tomorrow afternoon to talk business."

"That's right."

"Have you already thought of what you're going to do with your big bonus? I was thinking maybe we could take a trip."

I clenched my jaw.

"Are you there?"

"Yeah, I'm here."

"You don't sound well."

"Barry, I can't marry you." I winced, wishing I hadn't just blurted it out like that, but I couldn't take it back now.

"What?" he said, sounding floored. Then he laughed. "Denise…what are you saying?"

I sighed and summoned strength—I didn't want to hurt him. "I'm saying that I can't marry you, Barry. I'm sorry, but I don't love you…enough."

After a few seconds of silence, he scoffed. "You don't love me *enough?* You either love someone or you don't, Denise."

I swallowed. "All right then…I don't love you. I don't want to marry you."

"You don't want to marry me?"

"That's right."

He scoffed, making blustery noises. "I don't believe this. If you didn't want to get married, then what's with the wedding dress?"

I blinked. "How did you know about the wedding dress?"

"I saw it hanging in your closet the night I was looking for my toiletry bag."

And he had proposed the following night. I

brought my fist to my mouth as a horrible suspicion bloomed in my mind. "Are you saying you proposed because you saw the wedding dress in my closet?"

"Well…yeah. I mean, that's one big hell of a hint, don't you think?"

Humiliation rolled over me in waves. I sat down hard in a chair. "So…you really don't want to get married, either?"

"Well, I'm crazy about you, Denise, and we don't argue, and we have so much in common…I thought maybe it was time to just bite the bullet."

Bite the bullet. Barry was comparing marriage to me with sticking a gun in his mouth.

I was numb. My mouth opened and closed, but I couldn't seem to form words. Finally I managed, "Barry, I don't believe either one of us is ready to make that kind of commitment to each other."

He sighed. "Denise, I'm swamped right now. Can we talk about this later?"

"No. I don't think we should see each other anymore."

He scoffed. "Just like that? No explanation, nothing?"

"I'm sorry, Barry…I can't explain it to myself. Just know that this has nothing to do with you. It's me."

"You're making a mistake, Denise."

His words sent a chill through me. Maybe I was… maybe my life was just one long series of mistakes and missed opportunities.

"I'll send the ring to your office," I said in a

choked voice. (I hoped he could get a refund.) "I'm truly sorry, Barry."

He made some disbelieving noises, all under-standable—I was in a state of disbelief myself.

"Speaking of the office," he said bitterly, "don't be surprised if our breakup affects Ellen's decision to do business with Trayser Brothers."

I couldn't blame him for being angry. "I'll under-stand if she changes her mind. Goodbye, Barry."

I hung up the phone, took off the man-made dia-mond ring and cried. Sobbed. Really boo-hooed. (I never cried…*ever.*) Over losing my friendship with Barry, losing my heart to Redford, and losing my mind over love in general.

And I was in love with Redford again. Or had I never really fallen out of love with him?

In a torturous mood, I walked over to the cigar box of keepsakes and opened the lid, assailed by bitter-sweet recollections. I sat on the floor cross-legged and removed each item, turned it over, rubbed it be-tween my palms, wringing the memories out of each memento in an effort to conjure up my state of mind at the time. I closed my eyes, tried to push everything else out of my mind, trying to remember with all five senses.

I had been so…*happy* with Redford. Blissfully so…childlike. To the point that I thought it couldn't possibly last…it had to be a mistake. And it was. My judgment where relationships were concerned was officially abysmal.

My mother's parting words came back to me. *A wise person learns from their mistakes.*

Not me. I'd spent the last three years kicking myself for being stupid enough to marry Redford, only to turn around and almost make another mistake by marrying Barry. When I thought of how close I'd come to marrying a man who had proposed because of a lousy dress, I was nauseous.

The ringing phone roused me from my bout of self-loathing. I wiped my eyes and cleared my throat, then answered the phone, wondering which person I didn't want to talk to could be calling. Mother? Barry? Redford?

"Hi, it's me!" Cindy sang into the phone. "He called again!"

"Who?"

"Jim—the guy from my Positive Thinking class. Just now! We talked for almost an hour on the phone, and he asked me out again. Oh, Denise, I have such a good feeling about this guy!"

Her announcement roused me from my melancholy mood, and I smiled. "That's wonderful, Cindy. At least we know the man has good taste. And who knows—maybe he's *the one*."

She sighed. "Oh, I hope so. Denise, it sounds crazy, but I think I'm half in love with him already."

"Easy, girl," I said with a little laugh. But I knew just how she felt.

"Oh, gracious, I almost forgot the reason I really

called! I won the auction—you can keep your wedding gown!"

I dropped back into the chair, caught between laughing and crying. I'd forgotten all about the auction. I'd set this entire mess into motion when I'd made the mistake of buying that stupid wedding dress. Now after having Cindy bid like a madwoman to win it back, I had it.

Plus one fabulous gown—*minus* one fiancé.

My life was just too sad for words.

19

I WAS A NERVOUS WRECK when I walked into the IRS office Tuesday morning at the appointed time. I'd gotten no sleep to speak of, tossing and turning and soaking my pillow. I was racked with guilt over the way I'd behaved with Redford, and what I'd sacrificed—my relationship with Barry, my self-integrity. Even my parents knew that I had betrayed my fiancé with another man. That fact alone was enough to launch me into therapy.

But the basic truth was that my fixation on Redford simply wasn't healthy. Both times he'd rolled through my life, he'd left a wake of destruction. I didn't even want to think about how long it would take me to get over him this time.

I straightened my shoulders, focusing on my goal to get through the audit. I'd worn my most stylish suit in anticipation of meeting with Ellen Brant later; but sensible shoes since I was still hobbling from my foot injury. And after much self-debate, I'd also decided to wear Barry's ring to the interview…I didn't want its absence to trigger any questions from Redford.

Not that I thought he'd notice, but still.

As I shifted the box of tax papers, my mind clicked ahead to the possible costly outcomes. Since I no longer had an "in" with Ellen Brant, I couldn't count on the bonus for her account. If the IRS levied stiff penalties and interest for my mistakes, I'd have to sell my...what?

My wedding gown? The wedding band that Redford had given me? I could have a "has been" bridal yard sale.

And what if Redford had to pay a huge sum? What if it jeopardized the cash flow of his family business?

More than the audit itself, I was dreading seeing him this morning. Dreading the visceral response to him I knew was virtually irrepressible. A physical reminder that I couldn't trust my own judgment when I was around him.

I was well on my way to developing a migraine when I was shown to a small office containing a long utilitarian table, a few uncomfortable chairs and a wall bookshelf of imposing tax tomes—just in case they had to whip out a revenue code to prove their point, I assumed.

"Someone will be right with you," the woman threatened.

I set the box on the table and walked over to the window, parting the miniblinds with my fingers. It was the kind of cold, blustery day that made people hurry—trotting along, bundled in their coats and scarves, heads down. Redford stood out even more than usual as he walked toward the building, his stride long and precise, his duster coat flapping, a briefcase in his hand, his hat planted on his head, his chin level.

My thighs quickened. Even from this distance, he could affect me. I stepped back, and the blinds snapped closed. I chewed my last remaining fingernail down to the nub, my nerves ratcheting higher as each minute on the clock ticked by.

When the door opened suddenly, I was so startled I nearly cried out. Redford walked in and nodded to me, his face passive. "Good morning."

"Good m-morning," I stammered.

He set the saddle-tan briefcase on the table and shrugged out of his coat, then removed his hat. He wore dark jeans, a white dress shirt, and a gray sport coat. He looked so handsome, my heart ached.

"How was your visit with your folks?"

I wet my lips. "I told them everything, Redford. About the wedding and the annulment."

He pursed his mouth. "They must have been shocked, hearing it for the first time."

I nodded, clasping my hands together. "They were disappointed. I was raised very conservatively. It's not the sort of thing they expected out of me." I gave an embarrassed little laugh. "They think I'm Miss Perfect."

He shifted from foot to foot. "I'm sorry to be the cause of blowing their perception of you."

"I apologized for them seeing us...together. I

explained that it…just happened and that it was a mistake."

He glanced at my left hand. "I hope it didn't spoil their celebration of your engagement."

"No," I murmured. "They were…understanding."

His expression was unreadable. "Good."

The door burst open, admitting a stern-faced man holding a thick folder. He eyed us over half-glasses. "Are you Mr. and Mrs. DeMoss?"

I blinked.

"Formerly," Redford said, straightening. "I'm Redford DeMoss, and this is Denise Cooke."

"Adam Helmut. I'll be performing the audit." The man shook Redford's hand, then mine. His fingers were cold and stiff. "Have a seat."

Redford and I sat in adjacent chairs. When I crossed my legs, I accidentally brushed his leg. I jerked back and Redford looked at me, his eyes mocking. I knew what was going through his mind— Sunday night I had welcomed him deep into my body, and today I could barely touch him.

Mr. Helmut pulled out our tax form and reviewed a colored sheet of what looked like handwritten notes. After verifying our social security numbers and the tax year in question, he ticked through personal data and made more notes on the sheet.

"When and where were you married?"

I cited the date, then felt my cheeks grow hot. "At the Taking Care of Business wedding chapel in Las Vegas."

He looked up, then back to the sheet, writing.

"And when did you divorce?"

"The marriage was annulled," Redford said in a low tone.

"Ah. In what calendar year?"

"The following year."

The man nodded as if to say that he'd expected as much. "Do you have the annulment papers with you?"

With a start, I realized I'd left them tucked into my silly cigar box. "I didn't bring them."

Redford reached for his briefcase. "I brought a copy."

My heart thumped against my breastbone as the man so clinically examined the papers that had expunged our marriage, then made a check on his notes. "So the return in question is the only year the two of you filed jointly?"

"That's correct," I said.

"Have either of you remarried?"

"No," we said in unison.

He looked up, then down again. "Mr. DeMoss, you were a sergeant in the U.S. Marines?"

"First Sergeant—yes, sir."

"And what was your pay grade?"

"E-8."

The man seemed impressed. "Career man?"

Redford nodded. "I retired last year."

Helmut turned to me and verified my employment at the time and my address, which was the address on the form, then pulled out a calculator and announced, "Okay, let's get down to it. Did you bring copies of your original source documents?"

"I have them," I said, nervously pulling the box of papers close to me. When I transferred the stack to the table, the books I'd bought on Thoroughbreds and the Marine Corps and logistics were in the bottom of the box. My cheeks warmed to see my newlywed eagerness revealed. Redford glanced at them and a wrinkle formed between his eyebrows, but he didn't say anything.

For the next two hours, the auditor painstakingly reviewed every figure on every line, questioning every number, recalculating the entire return. My anxiety grew as we moved toward the schedule of deductions for my home office.

"Ms. Cooke, you were at the time establishing a home-based financial business?"

I nodded. "But since then, I've taken a job with Trayser Brothers. Most of my clients followed me there."

He pursed his mouth. "Trayser Brothers...impressive. Well, let's take a look at the receipts for these business expenses, shall we?"

My stomach churned, but I pulled out the documents. One by one, we went over the figures and I tried to defend the expenses for which I didn't have receipts. He frowned occasionally and made notes on the colored sheet of paper. The more marks he made, the more worried I became.

"Excuse me for a few minutes," he said abruptly, then left with our form and his calculator.

When the door closed, Redford turned to me. "How do you think it's going?"

"Hard to tell," I said, touching my temples. But I had a vision of Mr. Helmut gathering troops—a director or someone with police authority—to lower the boom.

"Redford," I said in a choked voice. "I…might have…fudged a little on the deductions I took."

One eyebrow went up. "You? Miss Perfect cheated on her taxes?"

I frowned. "Shh! This room might be bugged."

He laughed, seemingly unfazed by my concern, then gave me a pointed look. "Relax, Denise. Your secrets—all of them—are safe with me."

I flinched. He was telling me that he knew the real me, the me that I kept hidden from everyone around me. Only he saw past the facade of Denise Cooke, neat freak, compulsive saver, reserved investment broker. He saw the woman who could bend the rules, and occasionally break them. The woman who threw caution to the wind and reason out the window.

What he didn't realize was that he was the only person who saw it, because he was the only person who could bring out that wayward side of me. Strangely, relief sliced through me because I realized that when Redford left, he would take my dirty little secrets with him. And as long as I stayed away from him, I'd eventually be back to normal. And once this audit was finished, we'd never see each other again.

The door swung open and Mr. Helmut came in, followed, as I had feared, by another well-dressed man with impressive-looking identification cards on lanyards around his neck.

"Mr. and Mrs. DeMoss?"

"Formerly," we said in unison.

"I'm Stuart Stanley, the director for this field office. Mr. Helmut has just informed me of some discrepancies on your tax form."

My stomach pitched.

"There are *quite* a few deductions that are being disallowed."

My intestines cramped.

"But apparently, you weren't given the extra income credit allowed for military personnel overseas, during the time for which you filed."

My eyes widened. "I wasn't aware of an extra income credit."

The director smiled. "You wouldn't have been. The original tax relief bill for soldiers was so riddled with problems that some people were actually penalized for their status. When the tax code was revamped, the government mandated that the IRS review each tax form and apply the credit were applicable. It seems that yours, Mr. DeMoss, was overlooked."

He extended his hand. "Our sincere apologies. The credit will more than offset the disallowed deductions. We'll process an amended form immediately, but by our estimation, you'll be receiving a small refund."

I was stunned. And weak with relief. I looked at

Redford and he looked amused. "So are we finished here?" he asked the men.

"Yes," the director said. "Thank you very much for coming in today. The receptionist will sign you out."

When the door closed behind them, I looked at Redford and he laughed.

"Looks like one mistake cancelled out the other."

"Yes," I said, looking at him, my heart twisting. "If only all of life were that way."

He stared into my eyes and moistened his lips. "Denise..."

"What?" My heart thudded in my ears.

He picked up my left hand. "Don't marry this guy unless you really love him."

I swallowed. "You're a good one to be handing out marital advice, Redford."

"I just don't want to see you make another mistake."

Anger suffused my chest. "And what do you care?"

His dark eyes looked pained. "I love you, Denise."

His words sent a tremor through my heart, but in the back of my mind, I kept reminding myself that our reunion had been unplanned. Redford could have looked me up when he lived in Albany and hadn't. Wasn't that proof enough that his interest in me was fleeting and based on proximity...on sex?

"Don't say that," I said, shaking my head. "I don't want to hear it."

"I know you don't," he said, his voice low. "I heard what you told Kenzie yesterday morning. That Sunday night was just a fling, that it always had been just sex between the two of us."

I inhaled a sharp breath, but didn't deny what I'd said.

"Maybe it was only sex to you," he said. "But I'm not going to leave without telling you that Sunday night meant something to me."

I panicked and looked away. He was doing it again—mistaking sex for love. And I was dangerously close to falling for it again. "Sunday night... shouldn't have happened, Redford."

His jaw hardened. "Just like our marriage shouldn't have happened?"

My pulse clicked higher and I looked at him. "That's right."

"Well, maybe we should just call an attorney and draw up papers to have our night of great sex annulled!"

My heart shivered. Our relationship always came back to sex. I started gathering up my things. "I have to be somewhere. Goodbye, Redford."

He was silent, then after several long seconds, he said, "Goodbye, Denise."

I didn't look up as he left the room, not until after the door closed. My throat and chest strained to hold back the river of tears. It was for the best, I kept telling myself.

I love you, Denise.

And how long would that have lasted? Another six weeks, until we realized that we were too different to make a life together? I needed more than a few impulsive words to hang the rest of my life on.

I moved my papers haphazardly back to the box,

barely able to focus through my tears. I blinked rapidly to diminish the moisture and my gaze landed on the open file at the end of the table. The top of the colored sheet of paper read, *Reason for audit: Anonymous informant alleged improprieties.*

I frowned. Informant? Someone had accused us of *cheating* on our taxes? Growing more indignant by the minute, my mind sorted through the possibilities. A disgruntled client of mine? A competitor? A vindictive girlfriend of Redford's?

I scoured the paper and next to the word "informant" was a phone number, an area code that I didn't recognize, but that wasn't saying much. Overcome with curiosity, I wrote down the number, then shoved it in my wallet and left the building. I forced my mind to think about my appointment with Ellen Brant. There would be plenty of time this evening to cry over Redford DeMoss.

And tomorrow.

And the next day.

My nerves were still clacking as I climbed on a bus to take me back into the city. Thoroughly miserable, I dropped into a seat, pulled out my cell phone and called Ellen's number. If she were going to cancel our appointment because of my split with Barry, I wanted to know before I made the trip to her office.

"Ellen Brant."

"Ellen, this is Denise DeMoss."

"Pardon me?"

Appalled, I realized my gaffe. "I mean, this is Denise Cooke." Where was my head? "I just wanted to make sure we were still on for this afternoon."

"I spoke with Barry this morning, Denise. He says the two of you aren't seeing each other anymore."

"That's right," I said, swallowing hard. "I broke off our engagement. And I understand if that makes you uneasy to have me handling your investments."

"No, dear. Barry is a wonderfully talented man who will go far, but I have to admit I didn't detect any chemistry between the two of you."

I blinked. "Oh?"

"I rather thought the two of you reminded me of brother and sister."

I winced. "You did?"

She gave a little laugh. "To be honest, there was more chemistry between you and that yummy gay friend of yours."

I closed my eyes, but forced a laugh from my throat. "So I'll see you this afternoon?"

"Absolutely. And don't worry, Denise. You'll find love again. I intend to."

She hung up and I stared at my phone, astonished. Then, clicking with curiosity—and anger—I pulled out the piece of paper on which I'd written the number for the "informant" and dialed.

After four rings, I was ready to hang up, but then a voice sounded on the other end.

"Hello?"

I squinted, certain my ears were playing tricks on me. *"Redford?"*

20

"DENISE." REDFORD SIGHED. "I'm busted, aren't I?"

My mouth worked up and down. "Redford, what is going on? Are you on a cell phone?"

"Yep."

"I thought you said you didn't have one."

"I was afraid you'd somehow get this number from the IRS. You did, didn't you?"

"I saw the number on our file before I left," I said, my mind whirling. "What's this all about? *You* called and reported us for cheating on our taxes?"

"Yes, I did."

I touched my temple, incredulous. *"Why?"*

"Because I wanted to see you again. I know it was a dumb long shot, but I had to try."

I gasped. "You were in Albany for over a year and you didn't call, but you do this?"

"I can't explain it," he said. "I wanted to call you a hundred times—you were so close I could feel you. But I was afraid…ashamed. I felt terrible about what I'd put you through three years ago. I wasn't about to call you before my time in the service was up, be-

fore I could offer you some semblance of a normal
life."

I slumped back in my seat, limp with shock.

"Denise, I thought this audit would be a chance
to see how you were doing, and if there was a chance
that you still cared about me…that you ever cared
about me…with no pressure." He cleared his throat.
"Please forgive me. Good luck with your wedding. I
hope you're happy with your new husband."

I started shaking…just my hands at first, then my
leg started jumping, then my entire body was vibrating with revelation. Redford *loved* me. Had planned
this entire thing to give us a second chance, with no
pressure on me. Just another happenstance meeting,
like before, to see if the magic was still there.

And it had been. My heart vaulted in my chest. I
suddenly understood why Kenzie had been happy to
change her life, why Sam had been happy to change
his. Because anywhere together was better than anywhere apart. I would follow this man to Kentucky or
Timbuktu. We'd already wasted three years.

"Redford, you made a big mistake."

"I know."

"You see, I'm *not* engaged anymore."

After a few seconds of silence, he said, "You're
not?"

"No. I broke off the engagement last night."

"But you were still wearing your ring today."

"I didn't want you to know what I had done, to
know that I'd done it because…I love you. I love you,

Redford. I've never gotten over you, never stopped hoping you would…come for me."

"Let me make sure I got this straight," he said, his voice thick. "You no longer have a fiancé?"

"No," I said, my heart leaping with joy. "But I still have the wedding band you gave me, a great dress and two tickets to Vegas."

Then I had that bottomless feeling that I'd been too bold, too presumptuous.

"I'm turning around," he said, his voice breaking.

My eyes welled with tears and I smiled into the phone. "How are we going to make this work?"

"How do you feel about Albany?"

"Albany?"

"I've been asked by the government to consult part-time at the Marine base."

"But what about your family business?"

"My father will be disappointed, but it's more important that I be close to you." He laughed. "Besides, I'd still have time to look after a couple of horses of my own…if that would be okay with you."

I blinked tears down my cheeks. "Albany sounds…close. And good."

"We'll make it work, Denise. I promise you, after finding you again, I'm never going to let you go."

I was crying for real now. And I never cried…*ever.* "I'll be waiting at my apartment. Drive safely."

"I love you."

"I love you, too." I disconnected the call, feeling light-headed. In the space of a few minutes, my life had changed. No…my life had changed three years ago when I'd first met Redford.

I had so much to do! I suddenly remembered that I needed to call Ellen Brant and reschedule. I punched in her number, so excited I could barely see.

"Ellen Brant."

"Ellen, this is Denise Cooke again. I'm sorry, but I'm going to have to reschedule our appointment this afternoon."

"Oh? Is everything okay?"

"More than okay," I said. "I'm going to Vegas to get married."

"I thought you and Barry broke up."

"We did. I'm marrying the man I was with Saturday night."

She made a little noise in her throat. "Denise, I know you're on the rebound, but don't you think you're making a big mistake?"

"Maybe," I said happily. "And it won't be my first…but it *will* be my favorite."

Epilogue

LIFE DOESN'T always turn out the way you think it's going to, but it somehow always turns out the way it's supposed to. Redford and I flew to Vegas, (I am now a member of the mile-high club…er, twice) and were joined by my parents who, after the initial shock wore off, were very happy for me. Since Redford was making an honest woman out of me, my parents seemed willing to forget about the entire "making out in public" scene and welcomed him as my husband-to-be. In fact, he and my dad actually hit it off. (Who knew my dad had worked at a horse racetrack when he was young?)

Redford's parents flew out from Kentucky and brought his dress uniform and his grandmother's diamond ring, which was flawed (and perfect). The De-Mosses were delightful people who jelled with my parents amazingly well and immediately treated me like part of the family.

Cindy canceled her date with Jim from her Positive Thinking class in order to be my maid of honor— is that a friend, or what? But imagine our surprise when Redford's buddy Jim, who flew out to be his best man, turned out to be *Cindy's* Jim! They are a darling couple, I have to admit. And judging from the way Jim looks at Cindy when she enters a room, I'd say that wedding bells are in the cards.

And *my* wedding…ah, my second wedding was everything I dreamed it would be because I was marrying my first husband! We went back to the Taking Care of Business wedding chapel—it just seemed right—but were married inside this time. I was dazzling in my bargain gown, and Redford was gorgeous in his dress blues. When I looked down the aisle, and saw his face shining with love and desire for me, my heart was so full I thought it might burst. When we slid our wedding bands on each other's fingers, they were the perfect symbols of our love coming full circle.

Isn't life grand? Even the bloopers, the blunders and the slipups. Because if you never make a mistake, it means you're not living life to its fullest.

My mother once said that a wise person learns from their mistakes. I agree…but that includes knowing which mistakes are worth repeating.

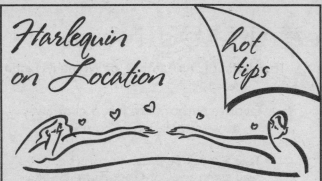

*Harlequin
on Location*

*hot
tips*

**Wherever your dream date location,
pick a setting and a time that won't be
interrupted by your daily responsibilities.
This is a special time together. Here are
a few hopelessly romantic settings to
inspire you—they might as well be ripped
right out of a Harlequin romance novel!**

Bad weather can be so good.

Take a walk together after a fresh snowfall or when it's just stopped
raining. Pick a snowball (or a puddle) fight, and see how long it takes
to get each other soaked to the bone. Then enjoy drying off in front of
a fire, or perhaps surrounded by lots and lots of candles with yummy
hot chocolate to warm things up.

Candlelight dinner for two…in the bedroom.

Romantic music and candles will instantly transform the place you
sleep into a cozy little love nest, perfect for nibbling. Why not lay
down a blanket and open a picnic basket at the foot of your bed? Or
set a beautiful table with your finest dishes and glowing candles to set
the mood. Either way, a little bubbly and lots of light finger foods will
make this a meal to remember.

A Wild and Crazy Weeknight.

Do something unpredictable…on a weeknight straight from work.
Go to an art opening, a farm-team baseball game, the local playhouse,
a book signing by an author or a jazz club—anything but the humdrum
blockbuster movie. There's something very romantic about being
a little wild and crazy—or at least out of the ordinary—that will
bring out the flirt in both of you. And you won't be able to resist
thinking about each other in anticipation of your hot date…or telling
everyone the day after.

Looking for a seductive cocktail?

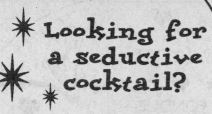

Try *Ero-Desiac*— a dazzling martini

With its warm apricot walls yet cool atmosphere, Verlaine is quickly becoming one of New York's hottest nightspots. Verlaine created a light, subtle yet seductive martini for Harlequin: the Ero-Desiac. Sake warms the heart and soul, while jasmine and passion fruit ignite the senses....

The Ero-Desiac

Combine vodka, sake, passion fruit puree and jasmine tea. Mix and shake. Strain into a martini glass, then rest pomegranate syrup on the edge of the martini glass and drizzle the syrup down the inside of the glass.

Are you a chocolate lover?

hot tips

Try WALDORF CHOCOLATE FONDUE—
a true chocolate decadence

While many couples choose to dine out on Valentine's Day, one of the most romantic things you can do for your sweetheart is to prepare an elegant meal—right in the comfort of your own home.

Harlequin asked John Doherty, executive chef at the Waldorf-Astoria Hotel in New York City, for his recipe for seduction—the famous Waldorf Chocolate Fondue....

WALDORF CHOCOLATE FONDUE
Serves 6-8

2 cups water
½ cup corn syrup
1 cup sugar
8 oz dark bitter chocolate, chopped
1 pound cake (can be purchased in supermarket)
2–3 cups assorted berries
2 cups pineapple
½ cup peanut brittle

Bring water, corn syrup and sugar to a boil in a medium-size pot. Turn off the heat and add the chopped chocolate. Strain and pour into fondue pot. Cut cake and fruit into cubes and 1-inch pieces. Place fondue pot in the center of a serving plate, arrange cake, fruit and peanut brittle around pot. Serve with forks.